TRAITOR'S SON

BY HILARI BELL

Houghton Mifflin
Houghton Mifflin Harcourt
Boston   New York   2012

Houghton Mifflin is an imprint of Houghton Mifflin Harcourt Publishing Company.

www.hmhbooks.com

The text of this book is set in Adobe Garamond.
Book design by Susanna Vagt and Carol Chu

Library of Congress Cataloging-in-Publication Data
Bell, Hilari.
Traitor's son / by Hilari Bell.
p. cm.
(The Raven duet ; bk. #2)
Summary: In Alaska in the middle of the twenty-first century, Jase is drafted by a
Native American trickster spirit to help stop a bio-plague caused by disruptions in the
earth's flow of magic, and finds himself in the middle of a shapeshifter war.
ISBN 978-0-547-19621-3
[1. Shapeshifting—Fiction. 2. Magic—Fiction. 3. Environmental degradation—
Fiction. 4. Indians of North America—Alaska—Fiction. 5. Alaska—Fiction.] I. Title.
PZ7.B38894Tr 2012
[Fic]—dc23
2011012241

Manufactured in the United States of America
DOC 10 9 8 7 6 5 4 3 2 1
4500343683

To my brother, Westly Kimbell Edell,
who collects 'em all. Even in Russian.

RAVEN FELT THE CHANGE IN the catalyst the moment the pouch left the girl's hand, so sharply that he feared she'd died. She'd put so much of herself into it, her sudden absence from the song/scent that drifted along the magical currents of this world was shocking . . . but it wasn't death he sensed. She still existed, the medicine bag existed, but she was no longer part of it.

What was happening?

If he'd had enough energy to change, he'd have hurtled himself into the wind and raced to see what was going on. But fighting off that last attack had drained him completely. All he could do was open himself, trying to feel every change in the catalyst's signature.

If he hadn't known the medicine pouch before it had bonded to her, he couldn't have found it at all — so at least his enemies probably couldn't find it either.

Because he was so focused, so rawly open to the contents of that small pouch, he felt the moment when another's hand closed over it. A human, not one of his kind. That much he could tell even from this distance. But this human's signature was different from the girl's, dull and dense, with none of the bright connectedness that had drawn him to her.

This one might be difficult. This one might be impossible. Most humans were. But he had to try.

If he quit now, this world would not survive.

CHAPTER 1

JASE SAT IN THE SMALL park near the border station's pedestrian gate, wondering if his father's client would let him speed on the way back to Anchorage.

Driving the most 'treme car ever made, he'd found there were three kinds of clients. The sane ones, who were dying to see what a vintage Tesla could do. The stodgy ones, who wanted to creep along observing all the traffic laws. And the liars, who happily urged Jase to make good time and then ratted him out to his father afterward.

Jase could usually tell the sane from the stodgy, but liars were harder. He was contemplating his dismal record at spotting them when the first shots sounded. And until the screaming started, Jase didn't even recognize the rattling bangs as gunfire.

He jumped to his feet, staring in astonishment as people ran from the line of cars parked on the Canadian side of the checkpoint. The people who'd been loitering in the park on that side of the steel-ribbed fence scrambled to shelter behind planters, or tried to cram themselves behind the big "Welcome to Alaska" sign.

The sign on Jase's side said "Welcome to Canada." Should he get behind it? It looked pretty flim—

More shots decided that question, and Jase lunged for the nearest tree. Diving for cover wasn't as easy as it looked on d-vid. The hard-packed ground was dotted with gravel, and his palms stung. His knees felt like they were bleeding, even through the fabric of the suit the firm made him wear to pick up clients. And the tree wasn't very big.

Should he try to make a break for better shelter? None of the shots were coming his way, but it sounded like a war had broken out on the Canadian side. Jase hoped, with a sinking dread, that none of the screaming people had been hit. The thought of someone in pain, maybe even dying, made his stomach twist.

Something scuffed across the ground behind him, and Jase looked around. More people were hiding in the park on the Canadian side, but there wasn't as much screaming now, even though the shots continued, accompanied by the breathy turbine sound of revved motors. It didn't quite sound like cars, though, more like the bulky hum you got from a big electric bike. Hogs? A drug gang? But dealers, of all people, would have enough sense to dump their stuff *before* they tried to pass—

Something hit the tree above his head with a loud pop, and Jase flattened himself against the trunk—no doubt getting sap all over his suit, but better sap than bullet holes!

Something rattled through the branches and fell beside him. Not a live grenade, which had been his first panicked thought, but a fist-sized stone. There was a gunfight going on just a few hundred yards across the border, and someone was throwing rocks at him?

Jase lifted his head cautiously. He saw the girl on the other side of the fence even before she started waving, because she was the only one who wasn't looking in the direction of the shots. Her dark hair was cut in ragged wedges — her frizzy curls didn't work nearly as well with the current style as his straight black hair. She stared at Jase for a long moment, then turned her attention to something in her hands. Was she tying string?

She wore biker leathers but didn't seem to be part of the battle, which sounded like it was trailing off. She looked up again, making sure she had his attention before she straightened and threw something small over the top of the twelve-foot fence. It lit about five feet from Jase, with a soft thump. Not a stone this time.

It was clearly intended for him, so Jase scrambled out to retrieve it, snatching it up and scrambling back a lot more quickly when another burst of shooting broke out. This time the shots sounded farther off; the nasal whine of the bikes was definitely moving away.

Jase looked down at the object in his hand. It was a medicine pouch, with half the beads falling off and leather that looked really old. Museum-piece old. Why would biker drug girl give him this?

Did he look like someone she was meeting? Or was this package so hot she was desperate to get rid of it?

She was now crouched behind a planter, ignoring him, which was probably wise. The cameras on top of the wall were in constant motion. They might have missed her throw, if she'd timed it right, but the more she ignored him the more likely it was the customs cops would do the same. And if that pouch held what he thought it did . . . he should turn it over to the customs officers, immediately.

He knew he should. But not all illegal drugs were harmful, and even the ones that didn't nuke your brain were worth a lot of money. Maybe a year's worth of car payments, despite the pouch being so . . .

Had any of those bullets hit his car?

o   o   o

Jase ran his hands over the midnight blue carbon fiber curves. He didn't see any bullet holes, but the showers he'd driven through earlier had left dust splatters that might conceal damage. He had just made certain that his car hadn't been shot, when a voice behind him said, "Jason Mintok? I'm Lloyd Hillyard."

The client! Jase spun and saw a gray-haired man in a suit that looked a lot less rumpled and dirt-stained than his.

"I'm sorry! I was waiting by the gate, with my sign and everything, when . . . Hey, you were on that side! What happened over there?"

The older man's smile looked tired. "I don't know much. We were sitting in line when a lot of shooting started, and both my driver and I lay down on our seats. A few minutes later lots of bikes whizzed past us, and then it was over. I heard some speculation about drug gangs, but I don't really know anything. The customs agent who checked me through seemed pretty upset, though."

"Did they get them? The bikers?" If they'd been arrested, would they talk about the girl and her medicine pouch? He really should have given it to the customs officers. A little late for that, now.

"I suppose they'll catch them somewhere down the road, but they're long gone at this point. The agents over there seemed more concerned with keeping everyone calm, and making sure no one needed medical attention."

The agents on Jase's side of the border had done the same—though glancing around Jase saw one man, probably a plainclothes cop, who wasn't reassuring people or managing the traffic that had begun to flow through the scanner tunnels again.

It was the man's eyes that gave him away, a cold flat gaze that inspected everyone, and then dismissed the person when he didn't find what he sought. He had the strong-boned features of a pureblood Native, and if that sleek leather jacket was as expensive as it looked, he made more money than Jase thought cops could make.

The intent gaze found Jase, who promptly looked away. This was definitely not the time to try to explain that some girl he'd never seen before—honest, officer—had thrown him a packet of contraband.

"Are you ready to leave, sir? We're already running late, if you want to reach a town in time for dinner."

This man looked like a stodgy, nonspeeding client.

"So we won't reach Anchorage tonight?"

"Not unless you want to get in at one in the morning." The cop was coming toward them. Jase punched the button that opened the roof, then darted around to open the passenger door. "We've got a ten-hour drive to the city. But you'll make that Sunday afternoon meeting with no trouble, I promise."

The client got in, then fell the last six inches to the seat, unaccustomed to sports cars.

"It's the low center of gravity that lets it handle so well," Jase told him apologetically. He was so accustomed to getting in and out of the Tesla that he forgot that other people weren't.

He put the top back up and started the car, swinging out onto the road. The plainclothes cop stood gazing after him, but he didn't shout or wave for Jase to stop. A clean getaway. Jase tried not to feel like a criminal. It wasn't his fault that biker girl had chosen him as her accomplice. And if that cop hadn't looked so scary, he might have come forward and explained that. Maybe.

Mr. Hillyard was looking at the thumbtack logo on the steering wheel.

"A Tesla? With tires?"

"The mark fourteen is the last Tesla Roadster made with tires," Jase told him, beginning to relax as they left the border behind. "All the later models are pure maglev. This one's just maglev boosted. It takes a bigger charge, but that's because it can use more power! It's got 375 pound-feet of torque, and . . ."

Mr. Hillyard's eyes had glazed over.

"It's already a classic," Jase said, changing direction. "My dad says by the time I'm ready to settle down and sell it, it will be worth twice what I paid."

Not that he intended to sell it, no matter how much its value appreciated. If Jase ever got that grown-up, he wouldn't recognize himself.

The client settled into the passenger seat, which was already conforming to accommodate him, and pulled the safety web over his chest. The magnetic locks clicked into place.

"By the time you want to sell it. This is your car?"

"Well, it really belongs to my dad's law firm. But I'm buying it from them as fast as I can. And before they agreed to hire me they made me take several driving-safety courses. I'm very safe. Really."

Jase set his teeth against the impulse to babble. If the client asked, Jase would have to admit he was sixteen and had only had his license for six months. But if he didn't ask . . .

Mr. Hillyard stretched out his legs. "Roomier than it looks. So where will we stop for the night?"

Definitely not interested in making good time, which was probably for the best. Jase's father had threatened to revoke his driving privileges for a year if he picked up one more ticket.

"We can stop at Tok if you want to quit around seven," Jase told him. "But if you'd like to run a little later, we could reach Glennallen by ten."

o   o   o

Mr. Hillyard was a good pickup, not unfriendly, but once they'd started driving, he'd opened his com screen and gone to work, which meant Jase didn't have to entertain him. And some of the curves that descended into the valley west of the border were a driver's dream. Jase had dropped down to the recommended speed limit as he swept down the hillside, as he always did carrying stodgy clients, but he still had to pay attention to the road. He didn't notice anything until Mr. Hillyard said, "What's that?"

That was a brown cloud hovering over the road at the bottom of the hill. Jase slowed a bit more.

"Dust?" He didn't see any roadwork.

The cloud swirled and surged toward them, resolving itself into thousands upon thousands of bees.

Nerves prickled up the back of Jase's neck. He slowed to a crawl, not wanting to coat the Tesla in bug goo.

"I'm glad you put the top up," Mr. Hillyard said. "Is this the right time of year for bees to swarm?"

"I don't know." Their small hard bodies pinged off the car's metal skin and rapped against the windows. "I guess. I've never seen anything like it."

Jase was *very* glad he'd put the top up. The bees were outside and he and the client were safe inside, but his heart still beat faster. He could hear their mindless buzzing over the swish of tires on pavement, like a distant chain saw.

Quite a few of the bees had landed on the car and were crawling around the door and the edges of the windows. Between the black and yellow bodies traveling across the windshield and the swarm still in the air, Jase could hardly see the road. Mr. Hillyard reached forward abruptly and punched the button that closed the outside air vent.

"Just in case. Perhaps you'd like to drive a bit faster?"

Jase grimaced. "I'll have to wash the car. Bug guts are pretty sticky." But he increased his speed a little as he spoke. "There's a drive-through wash in Tok, but it'll take a sonic scrub to get it really clean and the closest place for that is Anchorage."

Bees were bouncing off the windshield.

"Maybe you'll be out of it soon," said Mr. Hillyard.

If anything, the cloud ahead of the car was thicker than the cloud behind.

"I think they're following us."

Mr. Hillyard frowned at the spinning swarm. "That's crazy. Why would they?"

"I don't know. I used a different car wax last time, but that shouldn't . . ."

The bees *were* following them. Jase could see patterns in the cloud, brown wisps surging forward to cling to his car. He'd thought bees were attracted to flowers, but there was nothing flowerlike about the Tesla.

This was too weird.

"I'm going to speed up," he warned the client, and took the Tesla from thirty to seventy in about two seconds.

The acceleration threw Jase back in the seat, but he'd been expecting it. The bees hadn't expected it, and scores of small bodies burst against the windshield—emitting tiny flashes of light as they exploded.

"Whoa! Did you see that?"

Jase turned on the vibro sweep to remove the disgusting remains, and in moments the windshield was clear. Cleaning the headlights and grill wouldn't be that easy.

"Some sort of phosphorescence?" Mr. Hillyard sounded as baffled as Jase felt. "I didn't think bees did that."

"Me either." Jase watched the swarm in the rearview screen; the bees were still flying after him, though they were falling behind. Falling behind a lot more slowly than Jase had thought they would. Those bees must be going almost sixty, and he increased the Tesla's speed a bit more.

The client, he noted, made no objection.

"Maybe they caught the sunlight at just the right angle as they burst." Mr. Hillyard sounded a bit unnerved. "I've never heard of bees swarming a car, either. Do you have a different species of bees here?"

"I don't know." On a list of things Jase cared about, different species of bees were near the bottom. "Though if they're going to be a driving hazard, I guess I'd better find out." He looked at the rearview again. "They're gone."

But he kept his speed just over the limit for another half hour . . . and Mr. Hillyard still didn't complain.

o   o   o

Jase drove through the auto wash in Tok, though the Tesla wasn't as crusted with bug guts as he'd expected. He found quite a few places where the homicidal bees had given their lives to mess up his finish, but instead of the adhesive stickiness he expected, their remains seemed oddly dry. Almost flaky.

The old-fashioned water car wash removed all the residue, and Mr. Hillyard eventually stopped looking for more swarms and went back to his com screen.

His client's silence gave Jase time to think, and soon worrying about weird bugs gave way to speculating about that mysterious leather bag in his pocket. His first chance to examine it came that night in Glennallen, after he saw Mr. Hillyard safely into his hotel room.

Jase took a few minutes to go back out to the parking lot and spread a cover over the Tesla. There was no rain in the forecast, but he preferred not to come out in the morning and find his car covered with bees. He'd throw away that new wax as soon as he got home.

When he reached his own room, Jase kicked off his shoes and sat on the bed, pulling out the small pouch before he even took off his suit. Judging by the way it squished there was some sort of powder inside, and the girl had done a lousy job with her knots. The cords that had wrapped neatly around it had come loose, tangling in his pocket, and Jase had to unscramble them before he could tackle the final knot that closed the neck.

His grandfather would be appalled that anyone would use a medicine pouch to smuggle something harmful, and the old man had dumped enough culture guilt when Jase was little that his conscience twinged. But *he* wasn't the one who'd chosen that disguise for their drugs.

Was it time to try again with his grandfather?

Jase groaned aloud at the thought. Getting to his grandparents' house would take eight hours, and the last time he hadn't gotten past the front door! The time before that his grandmother had let him in. His grandfather had asked his gruff question, always the first thing he said to Jase these days. After Jase had answered, he'd turned on the TV and refused to say anything more.

But Jase couldn't change the answer.

His parents and his grandmother said that the gulf between his father and his grandfather wasn't his fault, but Jase couldn't help but feel things would be different if he'd been better at it, when his grandfather had tried so hard to indoctrinate him into Our Way of Life. He could still hear the capital letters the old man put on those words.

But even if he wasn't cut out for any of the Ananut paths, he couldn't shake the thought that someday he might be able to get through to his grandfather. They'd both tried, in the beginning. That had to count for something, didn't it?

It was time to try again.

He'd go next weekend, Jase resolved. Unless his father's firm had another job for him. He was trying not to hope too hard for that, when the medicine bag's strings finally loosened.

There weren't any drugs so powerful you'd get in trouble just touching them, right? If this was the kind of stuff that nuked people's brains, he could always flush it. He would flush it, as soon as he knew what it was.

Jase opened the narrow neck and looked in, but there wasn't

enough light to see anything. He tipped a small amount of the powder onto his palm. He knew nothing about drugs, but to him it looked like . . .

"Dirt?" The word sounded loud in the empty room.

Small brown crystals that looked like fine sand. Powdery dust that left a pale yellow smudge on his palm. It smelled dusty, not the chemical tang he'd been expecting. Jase quashed the temptation to taste it before he'd even stuck out his tongue. And he'd better wash his hands. Thoroughly.

He really didn't know about drugs. There probably was one that left yellow smudges. And it probably turned you into a raving imbecile with a single touch. And it didn't show any sign it was going to affect you for about twelve hours, so you started to believe you were a flying goat just as your car was doing sixty around a forty-mile-an-hour curve.

Because your car could do that.

Jase tipped the drug, dirt, whatever-it-was, back into the pouch and tied it closed. If they didn't even store it in an air-tight container it couldn't be too lethal, but he'd wash his hands anyway.

He didn't know about drugs, and he wasn't stupid enough to want to change that, not on a personal level.

But he'd bet Ferd knew someone who did.

° ° °

The next morning they set off early—at least Jase thought 7 a.m. was early. And it didn't matter that the sun was up, because this time of year it rose at four in the morning! Some Alaskans didn't seem to need much sleep in the summer. Jase wasn't one of them.

Fortunately the day was clear, with only a scattering of

clouds, so they might make it all the way to Anchorage on dry roads.

After Glennallen came a long flat stretch where the swampy icky woods were dotted with swampy meadows and swamps. Then there was a hilly stretch where Jase let the Tesla out just a little, because it hugged the curves so sweetly.

When you lived in the only state in the U.S. that didn't have speed sensors outside the cities, you had to take advantage of it sometimes.

Mr. Hillyard, who'd been silent all morning, finally looked up from his screen. "This is incredible."

"It's got almost no drift on curves," Jase told him, "because the battery weight is balanced over the tires. Maglev cars may use less power, and they can go fast if you don't have to worry about braking. But for real performance nothing beats tires."

He flexed his hands on the steering wheel. In a car like this the driver could feel the road's surface through the wheel, through the way the car handled.

"That's probably true," said Mr. Hillyard. "But I was talking about the scenery. That glacier over there is the third I've seen this morning. What's its name?"

"I don't know. Alaska's full of glaciers."

"The car's pretty incredible too," Mr. Hillyard admitted. "Though I'm surprised your parents would buy it for a sixteen-year-old."

If he was questioning Jase's father's parenting judgment, would he question his legal judgment as well?

"I'm paying it off," Jase said quickly. "He didn't just give it to me. It's got one of the best safety systems on the road, even today. And I have to keep my grades up, and pay for my own insurance and maintenance. Dad's firm has clients all over Alaska and northern Canada, with documents that need physical signatures, and more discretion than you can get dumping them at a small-town post office. Or clients who need someone to pick them up, discreetly."

His father had explained why this client had to come in for an off-the-books weekend meeting, but it had to do with proprietary contracts and competitors, and Jase hadn't paid attention. Most of the clients he drove had competitors they were paranoid about. That was why they let the firm transport them, instead of taking a public flight.

"You're doing a good job," Mr. Hillyard assured him. "I just . . . Does your mother approve?"

"Not really. But she . . . Hey, how do you know I'm sixteen? I didn't tell you. Do you know my parents, or something?"

When a client was also a friend, Jase's father usually mentioned it.

"I don't know your parents." Mr. Hillyard's gaze fell, his fingers fidgeting with the dead com board. "But I know about the lawsuit, of course. If you were three during *Mintok v. the Native Corporation Acts,* that was in 2081. So you'd be sixteen now."

"And three-sixteenths." Jase had intended to sound cool and nonchalant, but some of the bitterness leaked in.

"I'm sorry," the client said. "But surely that case made it matter less. Legally, not at all!"

The law didn't decide what mattered. Not as far as Jase could see.

"Of course, sir. We'll reach Anchorage in a few more hours. Do you want to go straight to the firm's guest apartment? Or would you like to stop somewhere for lunch first?"

o   o   o

It was early afternoon by the time Jase finally deposited the client, and then commed his dad to report, and added that he was going to stop by Ferd's on the way home.

His father, already dressed up for the client's meeting, said, "Tell your mother."

So Jase commed her too, then drove up the hill to Ferd's house. Flattop Mountain was less a mountain than a long ridge that formed the southern border of the city. His father said the view, which let residents watch the big freighters coming in to dock, added a zero to every house price. Jase's mother said it was worth it. Ferd's house was one of the more modest homes on the hill's lower slopes. On the top were mansions. Jase's house was somewhere in between.

He didn't have to com Ferd. He pulled into the driveway and beeped the horn, and several minutes later Ferd came out, hopping as he finished pulling on his shoes. He tumbled into the passenger seat as if he belonged there, then turned his wildly freckled face toward Jase.

"Bro, that shroud. It's just *wrong*."

Jase eyed Ferd's neon green stretchie, decorated with a rotating spiral of DNA. It appeared to be mutating as it spun. "The suit? I was working. Everyone wears a suit to work. Your father wears a suit."

"Exactly. My *father*."

"Oh for . . . I'll change later! Do you know someone who knows about drugs?"

"I know someone who knows something about anything," said Ferd. "Why?"

Jase drove to a turnoff, where they could park overlooking the city. This time of day no one would be nuzzling there.

Ferd's eyes grew wide as Jase told him about the shootout at the border station, the girl, the pouch, and his own conclusions.

"But if it's something harsh I'm flushing it," Jase finished firmly. "And if it's as new as I think it is, it's probably a nasty one. Because why disguise it in a medicine pouch, if it's not so new that the border scanners can't detect it?"

"Let me see. It probably is new. Designer. And if the scanners can't detect it . . ."

Ferd untied the pouch and tipped a small sample of the powder into his hand.

"Whoa."

"Do you recognize it? Know what it is?"

"Not a clue. You're right, it looks like dirt. A totally new drug. Bro, this is terminal! If the scanners won't detect it . . . Well, whoa."

"*Terminal*? What happened to *'treme*?"

"'*Treme* is completely last year," Ferd said. "*Terminal* is now the cool way to say cool."

"You were saying *'treme* just a few days ago," Jase protested.

"Then it's last week. Or month. Whatever. Focus in, bro. A designer that can pass scanners would be worth serious money!"

"We don't know if it can pass the scans," Jase reminded him. "She threw it over the fence."

"Was she hot?" This was a question that could distract Ferd even from money.

"Nothing special," said Jase. "And if it's a new designer, it's probably harsh."

"Not necessarily," Ferd said. "Buzz and Finn are designer, and they're very mellow. Riffle and Keloscope are new, and they're designed *not* to burn your brains out."

"I should go straight home and flush the whole package." Jase knew he should.

"Bro," said Ferd, "it's your *car*. I've got a cousin who's in college in the city."

"Can he tell—"

"No, but his roommate is a chemistry major. In more ways than one, Manny says. He'll be able to tell us what this weird dirt of yours . . . That would be a good drug name. Dirt."

∘　∘　∘

Jase agreed to bring the dirt to school and meet Ferd, who would provide a proper container and then get the stuff to Cousin Manny's roommate. "He's a chemist, bro. It's going to take time."

Jase dropped Ferd off and went home, where he finally changed out of his suit while he told his mother about the shootout at the border—minus the biker drug girl and the pouch. At least it explained the sap and other stains on his suit.

It had made the news, a biker gang and a bag of drug money that had somehow ended up flying all over the road on the Canadian side of the station. Despite all the shots that had been fired, there were only two minor injuries. No mention of a girl at all.

"I wish you'd commed," his mother said, her gray-green eyes serious. "I knew you'd be at the border right around that time, and I was worried."

"So why didn't you com and ask if I was OK?"

Jase pulled a stretchie over his head and felt better. Ferd

was right about a suit being halfway to a shroud, but the firm's drivers had to wear them.

"I almost did." His mother sighed. "But I didn't catch the news till evening, and your father pointed out that if you had been injured we'd have been notified hours ago. I'm trying to accept the growing-up you. It's not easy."

"Um, OK. Whatever."

It made her laugh and hug him. In front of the mirror over his dresser. And because some part of him was still thinking about the three-sixteenths comment, for the first time in years Jase noticed how much paler she was than his dark, square, undeniably Native self. That was one of the things that had made the court case so devastating—that he looked one hundred percent Alaska Native.

He *would* visit his grandparents again, next weekend, Jase resolved. Even if it meant putting off finding out about the "dirt."

By the time he went to bed he'd stopped thinking about his grandparents, consciously, but that night he had a Native dream.

An elderly Native woman sat in a grove of pine trees, the bushy kind that grew wild in the lower forty-eight and some places in Alaska too. The woman's smile was warm and inviting. Grandmotherly. Jase noticed that the hovering mosquitoes left her strictly alone. And given the antique leather clothing she wore, it wouldn't be because her repelvacs were up-to-date.

"Oh, carp. I know I'm feeling guilty about keeping that pouch," Jase told her. "I admit it. But did they have to send an ancestral grandmother to scold me?"

Her smile faded. "So you do have it. Where is it?"

"Look," said Jase, "if it's something that nukes people's brains I really will flush it. But if it's harmless what's the problem? Do you have any idea how much auto insurance costs for a kid my age driving a Tesla?"

She looked confused by this, but she pulled the smile back on with an ease that made Jase wonder about its sincerity.

"I'm not here to scold you, boy. I'm here to warn you. In a short time, if he hasn't found you already, you'll be approached by a very handsome young man. You mustn't trust him!"

"Is it his stuff? Is he a dealer?" The girl had no way to identify him . . . unless she'd seen him get into the Tesla and drive off. There were maybe a hundred Teslas in Alaska, but Jase's was the only one old enough to have tires.

"He's evil," the old woman said seriously. "He'll try to corrupt you, and ultimately destroy you. You must not trust him. Don't even talk to him if you can avoid it."

Evil and corruption were pretty much what drug dealers did. And Jase was about to become one? He should probably think about that, but for now . . .

"OK. But if I'm supposed to avoid him, it would be nice to know what he looks like."

Jase would gladly avoid the person to whom that little pouch really belonged—and who'd probably just shot up a border station too! But how could a manifestation of his own subconscious warn him away from someone he'd never seen?

To his surprise, the old woman held up cupped hands and a wavering image formed between them, like a palm-sized holo-generator.

"That's 'treme! Will it be on the market soon?"

The old woman scowled. "Look at him. Has he found you yet?"

Jase peered at the teenage boy who smiled between her hands. "No. He looks young, for a dealer. Is this a current ID?"

The guy in the luminous image looked only a few years older than Jase, but he was man-model handsome, which was one strike against him already.

"He's not . . . he's not to be trusted," the old woman repeated firmly. "You'd be far safer if you gave us the pouch. Where are you now?"

"How can I give you something in a dream?" Jase gestured to the woods around them. Though he was sitting in his own bed, which looked very out of place in this wild glade. "It's back at my house, anyway."

Tucked behind some half-full coolant jugs in the garage, where neither his parents or the cleaning woman ever poked around.

"Where is your house? Are you in Whitehorse? What's your name?"

It seemed to Jase that his subconscious should know that already. And her grandmotherly smile had evaporated.

"What's your name?" he demanded.

The way she hesitated before replying reminded him of the last lying client he'd driven. "Please, may I come to where you are? It might make this easier."

"Sure," said Jase. "Why not? And make what easier?" As far as he was concerned, he could go back to sleep anytime now. This nosy grandmother was beginning to annoy him.

For a moment he thought he'd gotten rid of her, because

the woods vanished and his own room appeared around him. But then his closet door opened and the old woman stepped out. She was still clearly a Native, but the archaic leathers had turned into jeans and a rain jacket.

"How come you came out of the closet instead of through the hall door?"

It might have been simply because the foot of his bed faced the closet, and the hall was off to the side, but she shrugged.

"I'd guess that's where some of your dreams center . . . unless the pouch is in there." She turned toward the open door, clearly ready to look.

"Hey! Keep out of my stuff. What do you want, anyway?"

She'd already lost interest.

"Not there," she murmured. "Not that it matters." Her gaze went to the window and she frowned. "It can't be that dark. Not in Canada, this time of year. Where are we?"

"It's not dark," Jase said. "I opaqued the window. And we're in Anchorage, not Canada."

"Alaska!" Now she looked angry, and it wasn't his fault. Whatever the problem was.

"Who are you?" she went on urgently. "Where is this house? Its number. I need the number."

"You mean the address," said Jase. "And I'm not going to say, because I don't want you in any more of my dreams. I'm going to wake up now."

He could almost feel his sleeping mind, fighting for awareness. He tried to help it along, but the woman stepped forward and grabbed his arm.

"Oh, no you don't! Tell me the number. Tell me who you are." Her expression was frightening-fierce.

"Ow! Let go!" Jase struggled against her grip, which made it hurt worse, and finally broke through to wakefulness.

"Low light," he ordered, and the bedside lamp snapped on.

His lungs heaved and his heart beat wildly. His blankets looked like he and Ferd had been wrestling on the bed, as they had when they were kids.

The rest of his room was undisturbed, the closet door still closed. Not that he expected it to be . . . That was a nasty one! He hadn't imagined a monster in his closet since he was five, damn it!

"Window clear," Jase ordered, and then turned off the lamp as the window slowly depolarized, revealing the brilliant twilight of an Arctic summer night.

Usually Jase had to darken the window to sleep. Now he simply turned away from the light and closed his eyes.

It was just a stupid dream. But there was no harm in leaving the window clear till morning.

o   o   o

He was drying off after his shower when he noticed the bruises, a row of dark splotches on the back of his arm where the dream woman's fingers had dug in. The sight shocked him, until his rational mind kicked in. He must have picked them up when he was diving behind that tree, back at the border. When they began to ache, he'd dreamed up the old woman to account for the pain, which explained the weird dream too.

It was odd that the bruises hadn't bothered him yesterday, but he'd probably been sleeping in a position that put strain on them or something. They still ached, as he put on the collared shirt and blazer that Murie Preparatory Academy required its students to wear, even in the summer.

He'd have to remember to get the pouch out of its hiding place before he took off for school.

CHAPTER 2

JASE DIDN'T HAVE A CHANCE to talk with Ferd alone till their lunch break. And since, as Ferd pointed out, trying to sneak off and find a place out of range of the school's security net would be more likely to draw attention than anything a student did in the cafeteria, Jase simply handed over the pouch and then watched as Ferd poured about a quarter of the powder into a plastic container with a simple snap lid.

"Stop looking so itchy." Ferd's calm voice cut through the high-pitched girl gossip more clearly than a shout. "With all that goes on in here, we could set our hair on fire and no one would noti—Hey, Ron! See you on the court, bro!"

Ron stopped to talk to them, and he didn't give the pouch in Ferd's hands more than a glance.

Jase looked around the crowded room. The same dress code that stuck them all in boring blazers demanded that face gems be turned off during school hours, but outside of class that prohibition was loosely enforced. Tiny sparks of color winked on most of the girls' faces and some of the guys'. None of the faces was turned in their direction.

"He probably thinks it's something for Culture Club," Ferd said, after Ron had set up their handball time and moved on. "It looks like something for Culture Club."

"You're not in Culture Club," said Jase. Neither was he. Three-sixteenths.

"The point," said Ferd, "is that if you act like you're not doing anything, no one cares." He knotted the strings and handed the pouch back to Jase.

"Why don't you keep it?"

"'Cause if it really is something harsh, with a heavy sentence attached, the less I have on me the better."

"Gee, thanks." Jase pocketed the small leather bag. "How long before Manny gets back to you?"

"A while," said Ferd. "His roommate's got some big project due day after tomorrow, so he can't even start on it now. And then he's got to arrange a time when he can have the lab to himself."

"You mean I've got to carry this stuff for . . . how long? A week? With its heavy sentence attached. I'm going to flush it," Jase said. "I swear I will."

"Close your eyes and think of your car payments," Ferd told him. "Then tuck it back wherever you're hiding it, and forget about it."

So Jase did.

o   o   o

Four days later he was walking down the hall with Rochelle, Mick and Tia, on their way to algebra, when the girl smiled at him.

Jase stopped. Mick and the girls walked a few more steps and then looked to see what had happened to him. Mick's eyes didn't quite bulge when he saw her, but they opened wide.

"Oh," he breathed. "Oh, wow."

"Hey," said Jase. "I saw her first."

"Yeah, but—"

Rochelle, who Mick had been trying to flirt with for the last three weeks, hit him in the ribs with her elbow.

"Ow! Why did you . . . ? Oh, um . . . Come on, Rocky, be fair. There's not a guy in the world who wouldn't look at *that*."

Jase had to agree. Gleaming night black hair fell past her waist, drawing attention to the curves of a body that was . . . wow. A single wedge of dark bangs over one eye called attention to a face that was almost as good as the body.

"Give them a break," Tia said tolerantly. "Guys have been walking into walls all over the school since she showed up."

"Easy for you to say." Rochelle glared at Mick.

"I didn't walk into anything," Jase said. But he was still staring.

"You would have," Tia told him, "if there'd been a wall in front of you."

"She's new," said Rochelle. "Just started today, and everyone's talking about her. She'll probably turn up in the Culture Club," she added, turning to Jase, "if you want to meet her."

It was like having a bucket of cold water dumped over him. Of course this gorgeous girl, gorgeous *Native* girl, would be in Culture Club. Where she'd learn that the boy she'd been smiling at was the infamous three-sixteenths himself.

So go talk to her now, the part of Jase's brain that ran on lust suggested. *Before she gets away!*

The rest of his brain knew better.

"Come on, guys," said Rochelle. "We're going to be late."

The Native girl didn't make a big deal out of it, but she

watched Jase as he walked down the hall. She smiled again as they passed her, but he didn't stop.

o   o   o

When Jase came out of algebra she was standing by the lockers across the hall, almost as if she was waiting for him—which made no sense at all. Girls sometimes tried to interest him, once they'd seen his car. Jase couldn't blame them. But if he wasn't in the Tesla, girls never . . . well, hardly—

"Hey," said the girl. "I'm new here. Could you show me where the cafeteria is?"

A lanyard in the school's colors hung around her neck, carrying a data chip that Jase knew held all the school's orientation stuff, including a map.

But her warm brown eyes were gazing up at him, and Jase decided not to point that out. "Sure. Why not? I mean, I'd be glad to."

Laughter stole into those big eyes, and Jase felt his face heat. So much for suave. But she was so . . . *cute* didn't begin to describe it.

"So, um, you're new here? You're coming in pretty late in the year."

He turned down the hall toward the cafeteria, and then realized that if he'd gone the other way, taken a longer route, he could have prolonged this conversation. Not that his conversation was so brilliant.

"It took some time to find your school." That impish smile flashed again. "But I'm hoping I won't need to be here long."

"You move around a lot?" Damn. Jase had been hoping to spend the next two years watching her walk down halls. He tried to think of something less sexist to say. "Is it your mother or your father who's the traveler?"

"Not exactly." Jase must have looked as confused as he felt because she added, "I'm trying not to lie to you. I'm trying not to repeat a lot of mistakes, which probably means I'm going to make new ones. I'm Raven, by the way."

That kicked Jase's mind back into function mode and his interest cooled. At least, on one level. "Boy, your parents must be serious culture geeks."

"Culture . . . oh. You think I'm looking for a nice Eagle boy?"

"Aren't you?" To this day, traditional Tlingit parents wanted their kids to marry someone from the proper, opposite moiety.

Jase's mother's moiety was Irish, which he figured meant that he could marry anyone he wanted to.

"Are you a nice Eagle boy?" Raven asked.

"No."

"Then I'm not looking for one." The smile was now so dazzling that if there'd been a wall in front of him Jase would have hit it. But they'd almost reached the cafeteria, and a different kind of wall loomed in the future. He might as well crash and get it over with.

"I'm Jase Mintok," he said, and waited for her expression to change.

"Nice to meet you. Can you tell me what's good for lunch in there?" Jase blinked. She hadn't got it. Maybe her parents never talked about politics.

"I'm Michael Mintok's son."

She looked puzzled.

"Three-sixteenths. I'm that kid."

Her puzzled expression was turning to concern. "I'm sorry, I can see this is important, but I don't know what you're talking about."

Jase stared. "You're really not from around here, are you?"

How could that be? Natives all over Alaska, Canada, and the lower forty-eight—even parts of Siberia—knew about *Mintok v. the Native Corp*. And she was clearly a Native, whatever else she was.

"No." Mystery replaced the mischief in her smile. "I'm not from around here."

She had to be yanking his leash. Someone had put her up to this. Someone particularly cruel.

"Did someone put you up to this?"

"No. It's entirely my idea," she said wryly.

Angry comments trembled on his tongue, but Jase managed not to blurt them out. If she wasn't setting him up, calling her a vicious bitch would be really stupid. But if she was setting him up . . .

"Here's the cafeteria." He was turning away as he spoke. "Goodbye."

"Hey! Wait! I want to talk to you!"

Jase kept walking.

o   o   o

It had settled the dilemma, but neither Jase's anger or his lust was satisfied with the result. Jase swiped his personal ID through the school's scanner and walked four blocks to a sandwich shop for lunch. When it first opened, Murie Academy had its own IDs, but kids kept losing them, so they converted to a PID system. Not that kids didn't lose those too, but the fine for replacing them included a DNA scan and was high enough that very few kids lost them twice.

Jase didn't see the girl all afternoon. He'd been so weird about everything that even if she had been interested she was probably avoiding him now. But even if she wasn't setting him up, and really was as phenomenally ignorant of Alaska Native history, politics, and law as she seemed, sooner or later she'd make the connection and dump him. Just as well to get it over with.

It wasn't as if he couldn't get a date. He could pick up a date just by driving down the street. It was only when they discovered that he wasn't as interesting as his car that girls finally dumped him and moved on.

Because no one could possibly be as 'treme, as *terminal,* as Jase's car.

His mother said he should try to get to know a girl, and let her know him, before he showed her the Tesla.

Ferd said that two girls didn't make a pattern, and the last thing any guy needed was dating advice from his mother.

It didn't help that when he came out of school that afternoon, he found Raven sitting on the hood of his car. Jase hoped there were no studs in her jean pockets to scratch the finish. Then he noticed how well the jeans hugged her curving butt and stopped caring about the finish.

A long moment later, after she'd stood up, held out her hand, and said something he didn't quite remember, it occurred to Jase to wonder how she'd gotten out of her school uniform and into casual clothes so quickly.

The stretchie wasn't as tight as the jeans, which was just as well. The note of patience in her voice told him she was repeating herself when she said, "I think I got off on the wrong foot with you too—though this time I don't think it's my fault. Can we take a walk somewhere and talk? There's a park at the foot of that ridge, with a trail up the hill."

She pointed to the west end of Flattop's plateau, where Jase knew there was a parking lot and a trailhead leading up into the higher mountains.

The cynical part of Jase's brain told him this was a blatant setup. The rest of him didn't care. He hesitated.

"Please? It's important, and it's already taken me too long."

"What's important?"

Thick lashes veiled her eyes as she glanced aside, then the warm dark eyes met his.

"I'll tell you all about it, if you'll come with me."

She was clearly concealing something. Curiosity stirred.

Jase pulled out his com pod and left a message for Ferd. "Canceling, bro. Tell you later."

He smiled at Raven. "I'm all yours."

"I hope so," she said. "It will make things ever so much simpler."

But she didn't sound like she expected it.

For once, the afternoon was clear enough for him to leave the top open. Raven didn't fall the last six inches into the seat, like his mother still did sometimes, but she didn't look at the dash with the avidity of someone who cared about cars. On their first ride, both Nia and Ressa spouted questions about the Tesla, mostly about how fast it could go.

"You're not a car person, are you?" Jase asked, turning on the motor and pulling out of the lot. If she wasn't a car person, why was she so interested in him?

Setup, a voice in the back of his mind muttered.

"I'm fine with cars," she said. "Though why does this one have tires? It doesn't look like the other off-road vehicles I've seen."

Jase snorted. "What are you? Some kind of space alien? This is as far from an off-road vehicle as you can get!"

She frowned, adorably. "Then why does it have tires?"

Jase talked about braking and drift until her eyes began to glaze, and then tried to think of something else to say. The speed limit on residential streets was low enough that conversation would be possible all the way to the trailhead, but the sight of her hair whipping in long black ribbons wasn't helping him think.

"Tell me," she said quietly, "why should I have heard of Michael Mintok's son?"

So much for romance.

"Why do girls always bring up subjects guys don't want to talk about?"

"Why won't guys ever talk about the things that matter? Come on. I can see this is important. I don't want to be tripping over it every time I say something. So talk!"

The smile that accompanied the command almost made it worthwhile.

"Michael Mintok is the lawyer who brought suit in *Mintok v. the Native Corporations*. You have to know about that. It went to the Supreme Court, and affected Natives all over the U.S."

And not always for the worse, whatever his grandfather thought.

"How did it affect them?" Raven asked. "Did it have anything to do with the dissolution of the reservations? I thought that happened about twenty years ago. You wouldn't even be alive then. And wasn't that about taxing casinos or something?"

Jase was so startled that he took his foot off the accelerator to stare, and the car slowed sharply as power ran back into the battery.

"Where did you come from? You can't not know this."

He waited for an answer, although he did speed up again after the car behind him honked.

"I could be ignorant for all kinds of reasons," Raven pointed out. "I could have been raised in a city, by parents who ignored their heritage. I could be the kind of girl who just doesn't care about silly lawsuits."

Jase was watching the traffic then, but she sounded like a total groupie.

"You're not that stupid," he said. "And you didn't answer my question."

"I'll tell you where I come from later today," she said. "And other things too, but I don't want to start that conversation now. So pretend I'm stupid, or city bred, and tell me why *Mintok v. the Natives* makes you look so grim."

It was probably safer than struggling with arousal while driving a high-powered car. But not by much.

"The dissolution didn't affect Alaska Natives," said Jase. She had to be from the lower forty-eight, or she'd have known this already. "We never really had reservations up here. What we did have was ANCSA, which settled the ownership of lots of land, including hunting and some of the mineral rights, on Alaska Natives . . . oh, about a century ago. They created village and regional corporations, and everyone who was at least one-quarter Native descent got shares in the corporations. The way it was set up, the corporations had twenty years to get themselves organized and running, to decide on policies and things, before they were able to sell their stock on the open market. But the villages got worried that too many people would just sell their stock, so changes were made to the act that allowed each corporation to make its own rules about whether or not to make its stocks public, and when or to whom people could sell it."

"So each village became a . . . a corporation? Jeho—I mean, that sounds odd."

"Worse than odd," Jase told her. "With every corporation making its own rules, things got totally crazy. Some corporations managed their resources, milked the tourist trade, and became as sound as any other blue chip stock. Several of them are blue chip now."

"What's . . . Never mind. Go on."

A city girl from the lower forty-eight might not know about the Native corporations, but she had to know about blue chip stocks!

"Just like any other business," Jase went on, "a lot of the corporations failed. And since the hunting and mineral rights they held became more and more valuable, they started getting scammed by corporate raiders. They'd buy one person's stock and then another's, for really good prices. The moment they owned fifty-one percent of the shares, they'd turn up at the next village meeting and vote to replace the elders with a board of directors who worked for their company. At which point the Native corporation became a regular corporation, in which a few Natives happened to hold stock. That was pretty ugly," Jase admitted.

His father said that people of all sorts falling victim to corporate raiders was nothing new.

"But all that happened a long time ago," said Raven. "Almost a century, right?"

"Yes, but after a few villages had been taken over like that, the rest of the Native corporations got scared and voted to put back the original ANCSA policy—only they said that no stock could 'be held, purchased, or owned' by anyone who wasn't at least one-quarter Native descent. Which meant that whatever fights they had would be kept in the family, so to speak."

"But what if someone who wasn't quite half Native married someone who wasn't Native at all?" Raven asked. "Their kids . . ."

"That's what happened in my family. Between Grandfather and Gima, my dad's three-eighths Ananut. And since he married Mom, that makes me three-sixteenths. Also eleven-sixteenths white, one-sixteenth Polynesian, and a final one-sixteenth Chinese. And it's kind of ironic," he went on, "because my grandfather's the one who's only a quarter himself. But culturally, he's one hundred percent Alaska Native."

He really should get out to the resort, and visit his grandparents this weekend. Jase sighed.

"So someone like you can't inherit your parents' property?" Raven sounded shocked.

"Before the suit, I could still have got everything except Dad's stock in the Ananut Corporation. He'd have had to leave the stock to someone else, who qualified."

"That seems unfair," said Raven. "Particularly if stock in the corporation and a voice in the village council had become the same thing."

"That's what my father argued in *Mintok versus*," Jase said wryly. "Along with a lot of stuff about this being 'the last bastion of racism enshrined by law.' I was three years old then. I was exhibit A. Dad won."

In a courtroom scene so dramatic it had been displayed on vid-screens around the world, because Jase's grandfather had been one of the chief witnesses for the Native corporations.

"Who is this boy, just three-sixteenths Ananut, to have a voice in my community, in my life?" he had demanded.

Jase's father had replied, "He's my son."

The shriek of wind and the whir of tires on pavement were the only sounds for a long moment.

"I'm sorry," Raven said finally. "But you were only three. Surely no one blames you."

"Not blame, exactly. Not most of them."

But there was a reason he went to a mostly white private school, and it wasn't all about quality of education, no matter what his parents said. And even in Murie Prep, Michael Mintok's son wasn't welcome in the Alaska Native Culture Club. That had been made plain before he'd even thought about trying to join. Not that he'd wanted to. Culture Club was all about Our Way of Life.

"Well, I don't care if you're Native, Samoan, or Swiss," Raven told him. "You're human. That's all that matters to me."

"Really?"

"I'm afraid so. Oh, turn in here."

Jase turned into the trail's parking lot. He had to maneuver a bit to get a view of the water, and in midafternoon with the top folded down there wouldn't be much of a physical nature going on. But a nice view set the right mood, and there were some things you could do even in daylight, in a car with bucket seats.

"It's your turn," said Jase, shutting off the motor. "What is it that's so important?"

"Walk first." The graceful way she wiggled out of the low seat distracted Jase for several seconds.

"Walk? You mean up the trail? Into the woods?"

"I said we were going for a walk, back at the school. Didn't you hear me?"

She was evidently a nature geek, wherever she'd been raised. And in Jase's experience, telling a girl you'd been too busy looking at her ass to pay attention to what she said was a bad idea.

"Sure," said Jase. "It's just that I'm not dressed for it. Shoes."

The school demanded dress shoes instead of gels, but Jase's had walking soles. He liked to be comfortable. And walking in the wilderness wasn't his idea of comfort.

"There are bears around Anchorage," he added. Surely that would discourage a city girl. It discouraged him.

"Just black bears," she said. "If we keep talking they'll avoid us. You're not afraid of the woods, are you?"

"Of course not." It was the things that lived in woods that worried him.

Jase raised the Tesla's top and got out. It didn't look like it would rain for at least an hour or two, so he threw his blazer on the seat before he closed the door and beeped the security system on.

"Ready to hike," he told Raven, and was rewarded when she set off up the trail ahead of him. She had an exceptional back view.

After what seemed like miles of uphill hiking, Jase was panting too hard to admire any view. He was beginning to fear he'd have to ask her to stop for a while when the trail leveled out to a grassy meadow.

"There," she said, turning back to him. "That wasn't so bad, was it? And just look!"

The view stretched over the basin in which Anchorage had been built, and from here you could look west over the bay as well as north to the ridge of mountains that rimmed the city on the other side. Jase looked northeast, to see if it was clear enough to make out Denali in the distance, but it wasn't. It hardly ever was.

"We've got pretty much the same view from our living room window," he told her. "And the living room has chairs. And no bugs." He waved off a curious bee, and then leaped aside as it zoomed straight at him.

"You're afraid of bees, as well as bears?" She sounded critical.

"I don't like pain," Jase said defensively. "It's called not being crazy."

"Oh?" Her voice softened to a sultry murmur. "No pain. I'll keep that in mind."

Jase knew he was being manipulated, but the promise in her voice lured him farther down the trail.

She chattered as they walked, pointing out flowers in the open glades and birds in the woods. On this rocky hillside the trees were thick and full, and now that the trail wasn't going straight uphill Jase had to concede it was pretty. But not so pretty that he followed her when she turned off the trail and plunged into the forest.

"Wait a minute! You can get lost out here. We lose a handful of tourists that way every year."

Those tourists usually lost themselves in Alaska's vast wilderness, not right next to Anchorage, but she was too new to the state to know that. Jase hadn't signed up for a cross-country hike. He wasn't dressed for it, either.

She turned back, framed by the dark green boughs, looking far more at home in this wild forest than she had in his car.

"I want to show you something. I can't do it here, on a trail where anyone might come by. We don't have to go far."

Her serious expression told him she wasn't proposing a bit of outdoor nuzzling. Too bad. Still . . . what was this important thing she wanted to talk about?

"All right. But I'm not going far. Not off the trail."

The woods seemed wilder out of sight of the path. She was quiet now, but Jase figured the noise they made thrashing through low branches would ward off any bears. He was about to call a halt when she stopped, at the edge of a small clearing with young, slim trees growing around it.

"Come look at this."

As far as he could tell she was staring at the ground, but he went and knelt to look where she pointed.

"I don't see—"

Something flat and firm clamped around his wrist and clicked, followed by another click. Jase stared at the magnetic cuff—the kind cops used—that fastened his wrist to the small tree beside him.

"What the frack? What is this?"

She couldn't be a cop; she was too young. And the police didn't need to haul people out into the wilderness to arrest them.

"I'm sorry," she said. "I promise I'll let you go as soon as I'm done. But the last time I did this my . . . audience took off running. I've already wasted days tracking you, and we're running out of time."

"I don't care if you're going to do a striptease," Jase snapped — not quite truthfully. He couldn't think of anything else she could do that required this kind of privacy, but her expression was wrong for anything sexual. Was she deformed or something? That would count as important, but he'd seen enough of her shape, even under the loose stretchie, to know it couldn't be too bad. "Let me go," he added more quietly. "I won't run off on you."

The impish smile returned. "Let's test that. In fact, I'll make you a bet. If you don't try to run, I'll let you go immediately and we can talk on the way back to the car. If you do try to get away then you have to forgive me for cuffing you, and listen to what I have to tell you before I take the cuff off. Agreed?"

"That's one of those bets where you get what you want either way." He was a lawyer's son, after all. "What about what I want?"

Raven considered this. "What do you want?"

Cuffed to a tree was probably the wrong time to say this, but Jase was too annoyed to care. If she got huffy and stalked off, he'd com Ferd to come out with a saw and cut the tree down to free him.

"Any chance you're going to get naked?" Jase asked.

She threw back her head and laughed, full and free. "I think I like you, Jase Mintok. Lord knows why. Yes, at some point I will be naked."

Jase stopped being annoyed. "You will?"

"I promise."

"Completely?"

"As the day I was born."

"'Treme," Jase said. "Go for it."

He was now watching with considerable interest, the cuff on his wrist almost forgotten.

She stood in the sunlight, smiling confidently. Then her face began to melt.

Her forehead and chin receded and her nose stretched out. An oily blackness flowed over her skin, and her whole body shrank like a deflating balloon. Her clothes collapsed around her as feathers sprouted, first the central shafts, then black vanes that grew out and meshed together.

Jase was on the other side of the tree, screaming, yanking on the cuff so hard agony shot up his arm.

A raven wiggled out of the girl's stretchie and hopped toward him. Two-footed bird hops, like a real raven. But it seemed to Jase there was more than a bird's intelligence in the round black eyes. It cocked its head and emitted a soft bird croak. He could almost hear the girl's ironic voice saying, *You lose.*

CHAPTER 3

AT SOME POINT JASE HAD stopped screaming, but his throat felt raw when he spoke.

"I'm dreaming. This is a just a nightmare, right?"

The scent of damp earth and warm spruce filled his nose. He'd pulled on the cuff so hard the edge of the plastic had cut into his wrist, and drops of blood welled around the strap. It hurt, even after he quit pulling. He was still shuddering. Raven . . . she'd melted!

"No, it's the drug! It's the dirt in that stupid pouch. It's giving me hallucinations, days after I touched it, just like I thought it might."

The bird hopped back to the limp pile of clothing, pecked the shirt aside, and dug its long beak into the jeans. It finally emerged holding a magnetic key.

The key to the cuffs.

"Don't you dare fly off with that!"

Jase felt stupid the moment he said it, for it implied that the bird was real. That the girl, Raven, had turned into a bird.

Jase looked at her empty clothes. At the raven, who was hopping back around the tree with the key in its beak. The memory of that transformation was horribly vivid.

The bird set the key carefully on a rock, then hopped toward Jase and croaked.

Jase stepped back, swinging around the tree. "Get away from me!"

The bird cocked its head again, at an angle impossible for human bones. Then it hopped back to the key.

And waited.

"You . . . you want me to take a closer look at you?" The very idea scared the carp out of him.

The raven's head dipped, just like a nod. It was big, far bigger than the crows Jase was accustomed to seeing—nearly eagle-sized. He had no doubt that strong beak could peck his eyes out, and its talons looked sharp as nails.

The raven stood beside the key and waited.

He could still call Ferd, but explaining what had happened was suddenly a lot more complicated than telling him about a psycho girl luring Jase on and abandoning him. If he was hallucinating the whole thing—which he had to be, didn't he?—he might as well go with it.

"All right." Jase tried to slow his racing heartbeat. "You can come closer. But when I say stop, you have to stop. OK?"

The raven . . . he would have sworn it nodded.

It hopped a few yards, then stalked the last few feet on scaly bird legs. Its feathers were glossy black, with white highlights where the sun struck them. It had round, solid-color animal eyes, and its beak wasn't shiny like the feathers. Slowly, watching him, it spread its great wings and held them wide. Its wingspan had to be close to five feet, and the feathers on the underside formed an intricate pattern.

"OK," said Jase. "I looked. Give me the key now."

The bird took another step, then stopped when Jase

flinched back. It croaked, and combed its beak through the feathers on its breast. Did it want him to touch it?

The thought raised goose flesh on his arms. Suppose whatever had done that to the girl was contagious? Suppose after he touched it, he started melting too?

"No way," Jase said. "Don't come any closer."

The bird flipped its wings and settled in to wait some more.

Clearly, if he wanted the key he'd have to touch the bird. And if he *was* hallucinating, there was no danger. Right?

Jase gave in and reached out tentatively to touch the feathers on its breast, wary for the first movement of that sharp beak.

He must have guessed right, for the bird stepped into his touch, pushing his fingers through the stiff outer feathers and into the warm down below.

Jase jerked his hand back and examined it. No oily blackness. No sign of melting. Yet.

"OK, I get it. You're a bird. Now can I have the key?"

Its body had felt like a bird's, thin flesh over bone under the soft coating.

The raven hopped back and considered him. Then it began to expand, rippling and bulging disturbingly as it grew. The feathers bristled, then contracted into blackened flesh. The beak receded, forehead and chin emerged, the neck elongated and thinned. Then the oily darkness faded into warm brown, eyelashes and eyebrows sprouted, and in moments Raven the girl stood before him.

She was completely naked.

Jase didn't care.

"Are you going to let me go now?"

"Not till you've listened."

She must have realized he wasn't watching her body, because she stopped posing and went around the tree to pick up her clothes. And for once, the part of Jase that couldn't help but notice all that smooth bare skin wasn't dominating the rest of his brain.

"If I listen, then you'll release me?"

"Yes." She started putting on her clothes.

"Then talk! I want to get out of here before . . ."

Before a whole flock of bird people showed up, and shot him with space weapons that wiped his memory and turned him into a drooling vegetable. If this wasn't a hallucination, he was pretty sure it fell into the "you've seen me so I have to kill you" category.

"I intend to tell you everything, but first, where's the medicine bag? I can sense that you're not carrying it—and you should! You need to bond with it in order to use it."

"What med—That pouch? That's what this is about? No, forget the stupid pouch. How did you *do* that? Who . . . what are you?"

"I'm Raven." She put on her pants and sealed them. "Just as I said. I haven't lied and I don't intend to. Lying didn't work out, before. And I've already wasted too much time finding you."

"That doesn't answer my question," Jase pointed out. "And I don't give a frack about the last time. What are you?"

"I'm a shapeshifter from a dimension . . . well, not exactly adjacent to yours, but we share the same leys."

"*Lays?* Like, lay of the land or something? How does that shapeshifting thing work? It isn't *possible*."

He felt more indignant about that than the cuff. Almost.

"*L-E-Y.* Ley. The leys are currents of magical energy that

run through multiple dimensions, which in this case includes both yours and mine. And you—"

"*Magical* energy? Carpo."

She pulled the shirt over her head, concealing a pair of breasts so lovely they were beginning to distract Jase from even this conversation. But mostly, he was still creeped out by the memory of that gross disintegration. Whatever she really was.

"If there's no magic," she asked, "how do you explain what I just did?"

"A hallucination," said Jase firmly. "Brought on by the drugs in that stupid pouch. Which I should have flushed! Or turned over to the customs cops. I could be in a hospital right now, getting that stuff cleaned out of my system."

His other theory had to do with aliens, who, after they killed him, would revert to bird form and feast on his eyes. All things considered, he preferred drugs.

The girl's eyes narrowed. "Honestly, I think you're going to be worse than she was."

"Who . . . that girl at the border? She knew who, what you are?"

And she'd still been alive when Jase saw her, which might be a good sign.

"Yes." The magnificent brown eyes were alight now, with indignation and enthusiasm. "She accepted Atahalne's quest, even though she had to run away from home and . . . hmm. Maybe I'd better tell you that part later. The leys have been—"

"I don't care about the leys," Jase said. "I'm too busy wondering if your spaceship can outrun a Tesla."

He'd bet the Tesla could give it a race . . . till the batteries died. Then he'd be at their mercy.

"Jehoshaphat!" She stamped one small bare foot. "You want to leave, right?"

Was that some kind of alien curse? It sounded like something an old-time miner might say. But the answer to her question was clear.

"Yes, I want to leave. Right now."

"Then pay attention! Your people have damaged your environment so badly that it's mucked up the leys. In all the dimensions, not just this one. The tree plague was the last straw, and my people are sufficiently pissed about it that they want to let the plague ravage your planet and kill you all. The only way—"

"Wait, the tree plague? But they say it won't spread out of the Tropics. It could never get this far north. And what do you mean, 'your people'?"

Raven took a deep breath and began to mutter. Counting to ten in alien? Or just swearing? After a moment she turned cool eyes back to him.

"You're wrong," she said. "That bioplague, which your terrorists unleashed, will wipe out most of the forests on this planet unless the trees become strong enough to fight it off. And the destruction of the forests will radically change the atmosphere, killing most of the animal life. Human animals. So you'd better start listening."

"I thought the trees were supposed to resist it," said Jase. "Scientists are surprised it's spread as far as it has."

He wouldn't have known that much, if his biology teacher hadn't been fascinated by the microbial war playing out in the planet's ecosystem. She'd talked about it at boring length.

"Exactly." Raven sounded pleased. "The reason it's spreading, instead of the trees fighting it off, is because the leys—"

"Magic leys," said Jase sarcastically.

"The leys are too badly weakened to support them." She was glaring at him now. "You don't believe a word I'm saying, do you?"

"No," Jase admitted. "Aliens . . . yeah, maybe. Magic, no. So you might as well let—"

"But you're the one who has to heal the ley! Atahalne, who made that pouch, he died getting it to the south end of this ley. And Kelsa—"

"Died," Jase said. "As in dead?"

"That was over two hundred years ago. But yes, he gave his life for this task. And Kelsa got arrested. She almost got killed healing it up to the border. She passed that bag, and Atahalne's quest, on to you! There's no time to find anyone else. You have to try."

"No, I don't. Particularly if it entails dying and getting arrested. Let her come back, and I'll give her the dirt and she can finish whatever-it-is herself. If you need to get her out of jail," he added, "my dad can refer you to a really good lawyer."

Raven sighed. "I wish she could finish. She was a magnificent healer. She opened four nexuses, far more powerfully than I thought any human could. That she chose you is an honor, Jason Mintok."

The way she said "human," as if she wasn't one, made goose flesh rise on his arms.

"Great," said Jase. "An honor. Well, I decline. If she's so special, let her do it."

"I can't," said Raven. "It's not because she was arrested; they've already let her go. But my enemies are too aware of her. They can track her, and stop her easily now. It was always a race, and they moved too quickly. They're still moving, but they don't know about you yet. If we move fast enough, you might be able to heal the rest of it before they can stop you. But we need to get started. Immediately!"

"Enemies? Never mind. I don't even want to know. Let me go." It was an order, not a plea.

"If I let you go, will you listen? Please?"

"I'm not listening now," Jase told her. "Because I'm not going to do it. Whatever it is. Get the key and open the cuff."

To his astonishment, she went to the rock where the bird had placed the key and picked it up. No difficulty finding it, Jase noted. Almost as if she really had put it there herself—which was flat-out impossible, no matter what he thought he'd seen!

She stepped forward and inserted the electronic key into the slot in the middle of the wide plastic band.

"I suppose instant cooperation was too much to hope for." She turned the key and the magnetic clamps popped open. "But at least promise that you won't destroy the dust in that bag. Or give it to my enemies. To anyone but me. It holds human magic, created for this purpose alone. I don't think any human now alive knows enough about this ley to re-create it. So it can't be replaced."

"Sure." Jase rubbed his wrist gingerly. The bruises were already darkening. "You can have your damn pouch back, anytime. Just keep out of my way."

He stalked back toward the trail. He could feel her eyes on him, but she didn't follow. Maybe she planned to pick up a ride at the trailhead parking lot. Maybe she could com someone to come and get her. Maybe she planned to fly!

The thing that worried Jase most, as he reached the trail

and hurried down the mountain, was that he half believed that last answer was the real one.

o   o   o

Hallucination. It had to be.

Jase drove home and hit the button that raised the garage door. Both his mother's and his father's cars were gone, but he waited in his car for five full minutes. If his . . . problem was caused by fumes the stuff emitted, he wanted to give the air in the garage plenty of time to clear. He was fairly certain it was safe, but he still held his breath when he went into the garage and dragged out the recycling bin. Jase picked through it till he found a plastic tub with a lid that seemed to be airtight. Then he went into the kitchen and armed himself with a plastic bag and a pair of salad tongs. Thanking God his mother wasn't home, he took a deep breath and entered the garage. His lungs were straining by the time he'd maneuvered the pouch into the plastic bag, and he had to run outside to breathe before he returned to press the seal closed, dump the whole thing into the plastic tub, and snap the lid down.

Then Jase went out to breathe again, and let the air clear a little more before he parked the Tesla inside. With the pouch isolated he felt fairly safe . . . assuming this wasn't one of those drugs that stayed in your system and kept giving you hallucinations weeks or years after you took it.

If touching the stuff had messed up his brain then it was way too late to wash it off, but Jase hit the shower anyway. Under the warm stream, with no more strange visions troubling him, he finally began to relax.

What the hell was he going to do next? He should probably have his mother take him to a doctor to get checked out. But if he did that, he might get arrested for carrying the pouch away from the border. If the stuff would pass out of his system naturally, or cease to affect him now that he'd stopped breathing the fumes, it would be stupid to spend several years in jail.

He should have known it was a hallucination the moment a gorgeous girl—a gorgeous *Native* girl—made a play for him. But it felt so real, so pleasant . . . till it turned into a nightmare. Why would anyone take drugs?

He got out of the shower and treated his damaged wrist. Holistomax was the best nonprescription salve on the market, but it would still be days before those bruises faded, and the marks would be impossible to explain to his parents. If it was winter he could have worn long sleeves, but in mid-June that would be too suspicious. Jase finally wrapped a bandage around his wrist, and decided to tell his parents he'd scraped it hiking in the woods with a girl. It wasn't quite a lie, and the girl part would explain the hiking part sufficiently that they probably wouldn't ask many questions. Any questions except Who is she? Is this serious? Will we get to meet her?

Jase shuddered at the very idea.

That solved all of his problems except what to do about the drug. Promises to psychotic hallucinations didn't count, but to flush the stuff he'd have to take it out of containment. And what if it poisoned the water system? If he buried it, some dog might dig it up and a kid could find it. And what was it doing to Ferd's cousin Manny, and his chemist friend?

Jase was reaching for his com pod to call Ferd when it beeped, and Ferd told him that Manny's friend had completed his analysis and wanted to see them.

o   o   o

Even in the Tesla, it took almost half an hour to reach Alaska University Anchorage in rush-hour traffic. Manny—darkly Hispanic to Ferd's freckled Caucasian—took them straight to the chemistry lab where his roommate, Georg, awaited them.

Jase had expected an acrid chemical scent, and test tubes, and beakers bubbling over open flames. Instead, the lab held a lot of scanner-looking machines and a bank of microviewers. It smelled of floor wax.

Yorg, whose photo ID badge said his name was Georg Ridders, was studying something on one of the viewers when they came in. "Ah, there's another! Thirteen thus far!"

"Hey," said Jase uneasily. "You don't have that stuff lying around loose, do you? I mean, suppose it emits fumes or something?"

Ferd cast him a curious look. Jase hadn't told him about the incident in the woods because, on the slight chance the girl really did exist, it made him look like an idiot. But hadn't some of the other kids seen Raven too? Mick certainly had, and Rochelle said everyone was talking about her. Unless he'd hallucinated that whole day? Was he hallucinating now? The thought made his brain boggle.

"You don't have to worry about that." Georg lifted his mild blue gaze from the scanner, blinking Jase into focus. He must have been using close-vision to enhance even the magnified image on the viewer. "No fumes. No physical effect at all. And it's still the most weird of samples I've ever seen."

"Weird, as in high street value?" Ferd asked hopefully. "I mean, you can't know about the physical effects if you smoked it, say, or—"

"It's not a drug," said Georg. "It's mostly sand, very rounded, more than what you see with most beach sand. The unusual part is the pollens! I've counted thirteen different species so far, and there may be more. But the most 'treme part—"

"Pollen?" Jase asked. "Like ragweed and stuff? Can that give you hallucinations?"

"No," said Georg. "I keep telling you, it's not a drug. But when I send these pollens through the biomolecular dater, I find that all of them are over two hundred years old! The small leather fragments in the sample are also from that same era."

"Um . . . does two-hundred-year-old pollen have any street value?" Ferd asked. "Lab value?"

"Not really. Oh, if you put it out on the nets some archeo-botanist might pay a few hundred dollars, but it has no value except for the unusualness factor. Which is high! I would have said that you could sell this pouch Manny has told me about to a museum, for an authentic medicine bag from the late eighteen hundreds should have some value. But the ashes mixed into the bag are modern, so a museum would ask many awkward questions about provenance and probably not be willing to buy it, since the bag has clearly been tampered with in modern times."

Late eighteen hundreds . . . assembled by a shaman called Atahalne? The fine hair on the back of Jase's neck was trying to rise, and he rubbed it.

"Could those ashes be from something that could cause hallucinations?"

Georg rolled his eyes. "Not. A. Drug. Get it? Human ashes, from the cremation of a man who died less than two months ago, according to the biodater. And how they got mixed in with two-hundred-year-old pollen and sand is very much a mystery. Where did you get this?"

Ferd looked worried. "Human ashes? Like, maybe someone murdered someone and burned up his body to conceal the crime? Can you tell who it was from his DNA? We don't have to take this to the cops, do we?"

Manny snorted. "Bro, if someone cremated a body to conceal the deed, they'd scatter the ashes, or dump them in a river, or bury them—not mix them into a little pouch with ancient pollen and stuff."

"Besides," added Georg, "DNA does not survive cremation. I'm doing chemical analysis here. This man—it was a man, by the way—had very late-stage cancer, and had been treated for it with modern medications, which did leave traces in the ash. I can't say for certain that cancer killed him, but if it did, it would have done so swiftly. But whose ashes were they? And why did someone add them to what looks to be an authentic antique medicine bag? Where *did* you get this?"

His mild eyes were alight with curiosity.

"We found it in a ferry locker," Ferd said. "On the top shelf, in the back corner. Like someone who'd used the locker before had maybe missed it. We thought it might have been a drug drop, but . . . No street value at all?"

"None," said cousin Manny firmly. "And no murder either, you freak."

"Are you sure there's nothing that could cause hallucinations?" Jase asked. "What about the remnants of the cancer drugs? If someone breathed them in, for instance. Or touched them?"

Georg laughed. "You're joking. There aren't enough toxins

in this whole sample to cause so much as a twitch in your blood chemistry, not even if you mainlined them. The pollen is so old, it probably wouldn't even make you sneeze. Well, maybe if you sorted it out from the sand, and snorted the whole thing. But I assure you, that's all it would do. The only thing of value here is the antiquity of the pollens—which could be worth a few hundred if you could find a buyer. And that's something I might be able to help you with . . . for a percentage, of course."

He looked hopefully at Ferd, who launched into negotiations.

Jase left them to it. If the stuff wasn't drugs—and Georg sounded like he knew what he was talking about—then what had he seen in that sunlit wood?

Georg asked to keep the sample he had, since he needed to work up a complete list of the pollens for any potential buyer. Ferd told him he could, as long as he remembered that they had a lot more of it and promised to cut them in on the deal. Usually the prospect of making several hundred dollars would have interested Jase almost as much as it did Ferd. But now . . .

Either he had a brain tumor that was manifesting in some very strange ways, or he had seen a girl turn into a bird. If it wasn't for the contents of that pouch, Jase would be comming his doctor to schedule a brain scan right now. But as it was . . .

Two-hundred-year-old pollen and leather. Just the kind of ingredients some ancient shaman might have assembled for healing a planet. Mixed with the ashes of a modern man. Jase had no idea how that had happened, but the combination was almost weird enough to make him believe . . .

Could Raven have been telling the truth?

CHAPTER 4

IF SHE HAD BEEN TELLING the truth, if shapeshifters and leys and magic might be real . . . well, Jase knew who to ask.

At dinner that evening he told his parents, "I'm thinking of driving out to visit Gramps and Gima tomorrow. Is that OK?"

His father's face tightened. It was a subtle expression—most people wouldn't have noticed—but Jase had been watching for it.

"Don't you have homework this weekend?" his mother asked. "I thought you had a break coming up."

"Not for two more weeks."

Unlike the public schools, which sensibly let kids out to take advantage of the summer and let them study in the winter, Jase's private school ran all year, with periodic one- and two-week breaks. Their only concession to Alaska's seasons was to schedule more of those breaks when the sun shone. Not nearly enough of them, as far as Jase was concerned.

"It's been a while since I've been there. And I'm all caught up with homework." He'd spent what was left of the afternoon making sure of that, since he'd known his mother would ask. "I'll be back Sunday evening at the latest."

One advantage of a driving job in a state where all the cities were most of a day's drive apart was that even his mother had become accustomed to Jase being away overnight. But that didn't diminish the curiosity in her eyes.

"Last time you saw Gramps and Gima, you said you wouldn't go back till your grandfather sent you an engraved invitation. And that was just four months ago. I'm glad you're going, of course, but . . . Wait, that girl you went hiking with. Was she Alaska Native?"

"Yes." Jase's face grew warm, though it wasn't even a lie, exactly. The blush only reinforced his mother's analysis, and his conscience panged when he saw how pleased she looked. She'd been trying for years to mend the rifts in her husband's family, or at least keep a com line open. She'd been upset when Jase said he wasn't going back—though she should have known he didn't mean it.

"Let us know where you end up for the night," she said, and then started chattering about a new exhibit in the gallery where she worked—to cover the fact that his father hadn't said a word.

o   o   o

The drive from Anchorage to Valdez took six hours, at the best speed Jase dared make. It was drizzling when he reached the coast. It usually was, and that was still better than in southern Alaska, where it rained all the time as far as Jase could tell. He pulled a raincoat out of his trunk and locked up the Tesla. The next water shuttle to the resort was due in twenty minutes, which wasn't bad, considering it ran every two hours.

It was a tourist boat, double hulled for extra stability, which was hardly needed in Prince William Sound. But the last part of the trip was open to the chop from the Gulf of Alaska, so

Jase found a seat in the center of the lower deck. He got seasick in anything worse than the slightest motion.

Despite the weather, most of the tourists crowded the outside decks, recording scenery and birds and whatever the captain talked about over the ship's com system.

Jase pulled out his com pod and tuned the small screen to an auto-tech series he'd been working his way through whenever he had time.

His school councilors were nagging him to start making career choices—and when Jase named his only preference, they promptly tried to discourage him with the amount of math and physics you had to know for automotive design. And it wasn't like Jase's other grades were better than the solid B− he got in math and science. He was never sure if they tried to discourage him because his father had hinted that he wanted his son to do something else, or if it was simply that graduates of Murie Prep weren't supposed to become *mechanics*.

Eventually the boat chugged into the dock, and Jase gathered up his stuff and disembarked. The area around the resort was thoroughly familiar, and his overnight bag wasn't heavy. He ignored the sprawling timber-and-glass "lodges" scattered up the hillside, and took the path that ran beside the tram track. Past the golf course—empty in this weather—and around a jutting slope to what the resort called an Authentic Alaska Native Village. The local Ananut called it the Disney Village—when they didn't call it something worse.

No one lived in any of the houses, of course, but even in the rain a few tourists wandered from one craft demonstration to the next, and all the shops were open. Jase considered stopping at the coffee shop, but with any luck his grandmother would be home to let him in and feed him. And maybe persuade his grandfather to talk to him calmly, for once, instead of demanding that Jase take sides. In a fight that had begun when he was three, and been settled completely by the time he was seven. His father had won. His grandfather lost. It was time they both got over it.

Past the Disney Village the graveled path gave way to a rocky muddy trail, but it wasn't narrow or brushed over. Most of the women from the real village and a lot of the men—all of them, when they weren't allowed to fish—worked for the resort in some capacity.

It had kept the real village alive, his father said. When his father was young, half the houses had been abandoned, with the village meetinghouse all but falling apart. Now . . . Well, it wasn't the upper slope of Flattop Mountain, but the small weathered houses were in good repair. Some even had modern glass in their windows, though the old glass wasn't that bad. One of Jase's earliest memories was lying on the floor in his grandparents' living room, surrounded by toys, with the heat of the sun streaming through on his back in a way polarizing glass never permitted.

His grandfather claimed the resort had completed the destruction of the Ananut Way of Life. It might even be true, at least in part. There were new restrictions on hunting and fishing, but it was a hunting/fishing resort! They had to offer their guests the best sport, in the best seasons.

The new village house, which the resort had built as part of the agreement his father had negotiated, had not only modern glass, but enough room for all the Ananut Corporation's offices, as well as the big meeting hall. The villagers must finally have accepted it, because as Jase passed he noticed well-tended flower beds around it, which couldn't have been planted by resort-paid gardeners. After the resort's first attempts to "help out in the local community" had been so furiously rejected, they'd fulfilled their contracts, but otherwise left "the locals" on their own.

But whatever the Ananut felt about the resort-provided village house, they hadn't changed their opinion of the deal that produced it. The rain was keeping people inside, so Jase had to ignore only a few hostile glares as he made his way down the street to his grandmother's house. *Her* house, by ancient Ananut tradition, so if she was home his grandfather would have to let Jase in. If Jase told the old man he'd come seeking a shaman's advice, surely a shaman couldn't turn him away.

As he stepped onto the crumbling concrete walk, his grandfather came out and stood on the porch, arms folded, barring the way.

Jase had been told that he looked just like his grandfather had in his youth, but Jase thought that if he lived to be a hundred he could never look as formidable as that grim old man.

He had to try.

"Hey, Gramps. I'm glad you're here. I wanted to—"

"The sport fishermen are out," said his grandfather. "So your father's masters told us to stay home. Are you prepared to admit he was wrong?"

Evidently, his grandmother wasn't home. Jase sighed.

"Do we always have to start with that? Aren't there supposed to be two sides to every—"

His grandfather went into the house, closing the door behind him.

"Carp." If he hadn't needed information, Jase would have turned and left. His love for his father, his own self-respect, demanded it. But Jase did need information, and his grandfather was the only shaman he knew.

He climbed the steps and knocked on the door. He didn't expect an answer, so he waited only a moment before he called, "Gramps, I know you're listening." He hoped his grandfather was listening. "Look, there's something I need to ask about. It's an Ananut thing."

The door didn't move. Jase pressed his ear against it; not a sound.

"It's a shaman thing," he called, a bit more loudly. So what if everyone on the street was opening their windows to listen. "And it's important. I need your advice. I wouldn't be here if I didn't need help, you stubborn—"

The canned chatter of d-vid came through the door. Jase gritted his teeth and tried the knob.

Locked.

Jase kicked the door, turned and left. He should have known his grandfather wouldn't put aside his grudges, even to be a shaman. Not for the traitor's son.

Jase stalked down the street, water from the puddles leaking into his shoes. He could feel the glares now. One surly old woman actually spat at him as he went by, and sneered when he hopped aside.

Jase refused to run, but he was alert for sounds on the trail behind him, and some of the tension went out of his shoulders when he entered the Disney Village, full of neutral witnesses. His pace had slowed by the time he reached the golf course. There were still no golfers, but resort workers used this path, and you never knew when a tourist tram might whiz by.

Jase checked his pod for the time—over an hour before the resort's shuttle arrived to take him back to Valdez, and almost two hours on the water after that. It would be late to start driving after it docked, but if he checked into a motel in Valdez he wouldn't be able to sleep, anyway. He felt like driving, late into the sunlit summer night, drowning frustration and humiliation in speed. After midnight, the highway patrollers thinned out. If he chose the right stretch of road he could let the Tesla out till the wind roared past and he could hear the turbine howl of the electric motor. It did make a noise when he really ran it up. Jase wondered how many drivers ever went fast enough to hear it. Maybe he would, tonight.

Jase sank onto one of the benches at the shuttle dock. The resort had put up a canopy, so he could pull back his hood and not get drenched, but he kept his raincoat on. Even in the summer, Alaskan rain wasn't warm.

He'd been there less than five minutes, when his grandmother came up and sat beside him.

She didn't say anything, waiting for Jase to speak, but from her it didn't feel like pressure. More like acceptance of whatever he did or didn't want to say.

"The speed of small-town gossip," Jase said. "Someone warned him that I was coming too."

"I got it from Helen, in the coffee shop," said his grandmother. "Or I'd have been home when you got there. I'd guess one of the shuttle crew called your grandfather. They're mostly off-work fishermen this time of year. Or their children. And he didn't call me either, the stubborn old fart! Your mother's not with you?"

"No, I came on my own—for all the good it did! He won't even give me a chance to explain, much less give Dad a chance! How can he abandon his own son over a . . . a political difference?"

"Not all political differences are trivial," his grandmother said. "The fact that it was his own son who broke the Native corporations, and then turned around and represented the resort . . . It made the whole thing much worse than if it had been some stranger. And he didn't blame you for it. He tried . . ."

The memory of camping in bug-filled woods, being hideously seasick in a fishing boat that tossed like a cork on the Arctic Ocean, and dozens of feasts, dances, and ceremonies in the village house rose up between them. Jase had been uncomfortable and embarrassed in turn, until one day . . . He'd been, what, twelve? Thirteen? One day he'd made some gaffe in the meeting hall, which he still didn't understand, and his grandfather had explained for what felt like the hundredth time that Jase was "one of the lost ones," and his grandfather was going to heal his spirit and make him whole. Jase's temper finally snapped. At least he'd had the sense to drag his grandfather outside before he told him that he wasn't "lost" at all. That his father had been right. That it was ridiculous to live in the Stone Age when you had other choices.

Later, after his grandfather had called his mother to come pick him up, Jase had tried to point out that the resort had poured money into the area, and provided people with more paths than they'd had before.

"The only paths he can see are the ancient ones," he told his grandmother bitterly. "And if you can't allow new paths to be created, then Dad's right and it's time to abandon the whole thing for a good career and a—"

"A life in the real world," his grandmother finished. "You shouldn't be afraid to say it to me, love. I've been listening to your father and grandfather fight since your father was your age. Younger! But the problem wasn't that your grandfather couldn't expand the old beliefs to take in modern choices. It's that he wanted his son to take the shaman's path too. And your father is a trader."

"I suppose that's one way to think of a lawyer," Jase admitted.

"All the paths have different aspects, different branches." A weary note crept into his grandmother's voice. "He was so set on his son's becoming a shaman, he wouldn't even teach him the proper way of the trader. If he had . . ."

"Dad would have been an even sharper lawyer than he is," Jase said, hoping to lighten her mood. "I know what they said about Ananut traders: If you see one coming, hold on to your trade goods with both hands!"

His grandmother laughed. "I was thinking about the other one, that an Ananut trader will clean you out faster than a whole pack of squirrels. But that's not the truth. Do you know the first rule of the trader path?"

"No."

"It's that a good trade must respect the craftsmen's work, on both sides, so everyone leaves the deal proud and satisfied. It's balanced. Equal. The best traders could walk around the entire trade circle, coming home without a single item they left with, but the value would be exactly equal. Because if you came back with goods that were more valuable, you insulted the craftsmen whose goods you'd set out with, implying the craftsmen of other tribes did better work. And if you came back with lesser value, that implied the trade goods your own people made were so shoddy you practically had to give them away!"

"So, this way, whatever he brought back, the trader claimed the value was equal? Because no craftsman would ever admit that other people did better work. So no matter what he came back with, no one bitched at the trader."

"No one ever claimed the Ananut traders were stupid." Laughter glinted in the old dark eyes. "And who can really say if a sharp halibut hook is more valuable than a good pair of boots? Or a satchel of dried salmon worth more or less than a bladder of seal oil? But the part about the trade being balanced . . . Your father never learned that."

"Lawyers don't do balance," said Jase. "It's the system as a whole that's supposed to provide that, by having a lawyer on each side."

His father had told his grandfather, over and over, that the Ananut corporation needed a better lawyer.

"But you let me in, anyway," Jase went on. "You let Mom in."

"I'd let your father in, if he'd overcome his own stubborn pride and come home," said his grandmother. "They're very alike, in that way."

They were. Jase sighed.

"Why did you come?" his grandmother asked. "After the last time, I thought it would be at least six months before you came back. And Helen said that Nadia said you were shouting something about 'shaman business.' I thought you thought that kind of thing was . . . quaint."

"I did. I do! But . . . Gima, did those old Native shamans have some sort of magic? Really?"

He felt ridiculous just asking the question, in the modern rainy reality of the shuttle dock.

His grandmother was silent for a moment. Then she said, "My grandmother, your great-great-grandmother, could whis-

tle for wind. I saw her do it, when I was a girl, out berry-
ing. We'd climbed the hill behind the village to that big berry
patch. I took you there once, remember?"

Jase did. He'd been stung by a bee and rubbed a blister on
his heel.

"She brought a blanket," his grandmother continued, "and
four big plastic buckets. All of us, me and Leah and Janny
and your great-uncle Arthur, we picked and picked. When the
buckets were full, she spread out the blanket and made us sit
on the corners to hold it, even though there was no wind. It
was one of those misty days, when the fog drifts and everything is still."

The patter of rain on the canopy sounded very loud.

"Then she began to whistle," his grandmother said. "Not
the sharp whistle you use to call someone back from the
beach, but soft and breathy. The notes went up and down,
very simple. But the wind came. First it ruffled my bangs.
Then it began to blow harder and we all put on our jackets,
and Arthur put his hands over his ears to keep them warm.
Janny's ponytail got all tangled, and later, when Mother was
combing it out, she said that Grandee did it."

His grandmother smiled, but the wonder was there in her
eyes.

"When the wind was very strong, strong enough to make
my jacket whip, she lifted up the buckets we'd filled and poured
out the berries, and as they fell the wind blew all the leaves and
bugs and twigs away, so only the hard round berries fell to
the blanket. After she'd spilled out the last bucket she stopped
whistling, and the wind died away. And we poured the berries
out of the blanket and back into the buckets, and went home

and froze them. Later, my mother and Aunt Mishka made them into jam. She was an old woman, and I was only four, but I remember."

If anyone else had told that story Jase wouldn't have believed it. His grandmother . . .

"Thanks, Gima. That helps. That helps a lot."

She smiled and let the silence return. She was better at silence than Jase, and a moment later he started talking about how his parents were doing, and asked about her knitting co-op. She asked him about school, about his driving job, and if he'd paid off "that car" yet.

But all the while, the back of Jase's mind was assimilating the fact that if Native magic was real, if their wise women could summon the wind, if their spirits could shift from girl to bird and back again—then maybe Raven was telling the truth. And if she was . . .

He wanted no part of it.

o o o

It was just past noon the next day, and the sun was shining down on Anchorage, when Jase pulled into his own driveway. He'd finally stopped driving and taken a room at Tok, but he'd still had trouble sleeping. When he wasn't carrying on an imaginary argument with his grandfather (in which the old man was forced to admit he was wrong on every point) Jase thought about Raven.

If magic really existed, could she be telling the truth about the rest of it?

Alien shapeshifters, at war with his own world over . . . What was it? Leys?

Jase had been so shocked by her transformation, he hadn't

paid enough attention to what she'd said. And even if Gima's grandmother could whistle up the wind, that didn't mean there really were shapeshifters. From another dimension, that shared rivers of magical power with this world. Right.

Maybe she'd hypnotized him?

After a restless night, from which he woke way earlier than he'd wanted to, Jase resolved again to let the whole thing go.

Which didn't stop adrenaline from slamming into his bloodstream when Raven stepped around the side of his garage and waited for him to pull the car up.

He had to stop to raise the garage door, and on a day this beautiful the top was down.

"Where have you been?" Exasperation poured off her in waves. And where he went was none of her business. Jase didn't owe her any explanations. But as she leaned over the passenger door, he couldn't help but notice that her top was both tighter and lower cut than the others she'd worn.

"I thought I'd give you a night to think it over," she continued with less heat. "And that maybe we should talk somewhere quieter than your school. But when I got here the next morning you'd vanished! I've been checking back since yesterday."

"My parents will be here," Jase said. His heart was pounding. Fear? Or something else, mixed with it.

"They left about an hour ago," she said. "With a couple of tall bags of shiny metal rods, with thick blades on the ends."

"Golf clubs." The fact that she didn't seem to know what they were added weight on the alien side of the scale, and despite his wariness, Jase's curiosity roused. He put the garage door up and saw that his mom's car and both parents' golf bags were gone.

Raven stood away from the car as he drove in and parked.

He kept an eye on her in the rear-vision projector, and saw that although she took a step toward the garage, she didn't follow him in. He could put the door down. Escape into the locked house.

She was giving him the choice.

That made up his mind, and he turned the motor off and came back out into the sunlight where she waited.

"Follow me." He led her around the house and up the steps to the deck. Even an alien-shapeshifter-hypnotist had to stop a moment to take in the view.

"It's gorgeous at night too," Jase told her, as she gazed out over the basin that held the city. "The lights spread out like a . . . a glowing carpet."

That hadn't come out as beautiful as it was, but he couldn't think of a better way to say it. He sat down on one of the shaded benches and waited for her.

"I saw it last night," she said. "It looks even bigger then. And for its size, it's astonishingly clean. For most of your history, a city half that size would have been a cesspool. Or a toxic furnace."

She sounded as if she'd seen those cities herself, and Jase's skin prickled.

"You're not, like, immortal or something. Are you?"

"No." She smiled at that and came to sit beside him. "I can die. Beyond that, it gets complicated. But I wanted to explain, now that you've had some time to adjust to the idea, why healing the leys matters so much. To both your world and mine."

She didn't look like an alien, smiling at him from the other side of the bench.

"Do you really come from another world?" Jase held her

gaze steadily as he spoke. Though if she was an alien, would he be able to tell if she was lying?

"Yes."

"What's it like?"

She sighed. "In some ways much like this one, in others utterly different. But what I said about the leys being vital to its survival, that was true. And they're vital to your survival too! If they're not healed, that tree plague your terrorists started won't stop spreading. And you know what will happen then."

"They're not my terrorists," said Jase. "And no one knows for certain what the tree plague will do. We've survived ecological disasters before."

Raven's brows snapped together. "Those disasters are a large part of what damaged the leys so badly in the first place! How can you be so . . ."

She took a deep breath and brought the smile back. "I'm sorry. You modern humans were trying to mend the damage, before this plague got loose. That's the exact point I keep trying to make to the others."

"Others?" Jase asked. "Those enemies you were talking about?"

For an alien, she had a really nice smile.

"Some of them. One of the ways our world is like yours is that we have politics too," Raven said ruefully. "Not elections or that kind of thing, but . . ."

"People politics," Jase helped her out.

"Exactly. And that's why it's so important for you to heal the leys."

"So heal them," said Jase. "I won't stop you. If you have enough magic, or whatever, to change shape, you've got to be able to heal stuff better than I can."

There, that got him out of it. It was true, too.

"Unfortunately," said Raven, with another of those warm smiles, "that's where the problems come in. You need to understand, the others' point of view is that humans have been poisoning these leys, on which our world depends, for centuries. In the last few centuries it was acute, and we were forced to expend our own power like crazy just to make up for some of what you were doing. And our power isn't infinite, any more than yours is. The power we spent cleaning up after you could have gone to serve other needs, and the higher the price of the cleanup went, the angrier everyone got about humans and your world. Then it got better, for a short time, but this tree plague was the last straw. A lot of my people really want to see humans destroy themselves, even if it means weakening the leys still further. They say it's so you can't keep doing it, over and over forever. But really, it's anger over the past as well. Some of them feel very strongly on the subject."

Jase shivered. A bunch of powerful aliens, hating all humanity, had never turned out well in any d-vid he'd seen.

Raven moved to sit closer, sharing her warmth as she looked at the bustling city. Ships moved smoothly in and out of the harbor, and Jase could see traffic on the highway.

"But you said you were here to heal the leys," he protested.

"No, I've been given permission to help *humans* heal them. Using your own power, for my people have refused to spend even a spark of ley power for this. Or to let me use it, either! If I so much as touch the leys, they'll shut me down. The only good news is that the others aren't allowed to use ley power to stop us. If we started draining the leys to fight each other, that might cause the very collapse I'm here to prevent."

Her hip pressed against his. It was cool in the shade. Jase, ever so casually, put his arm around her shoulders. He knew he should be concentrating on these alien power struggles, but leys and politics were beginning to seem kind of . . . abstract.

"But I've seen you change shape," he said. "If you can use power to do that, why not use it to heal, or whatever?"

She hadn't pulled away from his arm. That was good.

"Oh, I can use my own energy, the energy all life possesses. I just can't tap into the ley. But if you'll let me, I can teach you to do it! And if humans can heal just this one ley, from the upwelling to the terminal node, then they'll have to concede that I've proved my point, that humans can clean up the mess they've made. And they'll leave me in peace to get it done! Humans can fix this, I know they can! If I'm only allowed to show them how."

Her eyes shone with enthusiasm.

"But I don't have any magic," Jase said. "I mean, I'd like to help, but you've picked the wrong guy. You want a shaman, like my grandfather."

He didn't want her to want anyone else. Her soft body snuggled against him, and his arm tightened on her shoulders.

"But the medicine pouch came to you," Raven murmured. She was so close that her breath warmed his lips. "You can help me. I know you can. If you want to."

Jase wanted to. He wanted to do anything she wanted, starting with the kiss she so clearly . . . wanted. But did she want to kiss him because she wanted to? Or because she wanted him to heal the leys?

He pulled back and gazed down at her face. Her lips were half parted in invitation, but the flickering glance from under her lashes held more calculation than romance.

"You're trying to seduce me."

He was almost too surprised to feel outrage. No one had ever tried to seduce him before. It had all gone the other way. If his awkward attempts to interest girls could even be called seduction.

"You're trying to use . . . use . . . to manipulate me into doing what you want!"

He shrugged out of her arms and stood, staring down at her. Outrage was arriving, right on schedule. Anger came with it.

"I need you to like me," Raven pointed out, with a calm that struck him as utterly alien. "Ordinarily I wouldn't push you so fast, but my enemies are trying to find you too. And once they do, we're out of time. This is something most humans respond well to, so I thought I'd give it a—"

"Most humans? You've done this before?"

He should have remembered that this was the girl who'd melted in front of his eyes.

"No, don't answer that. I don't care how many men you've seduced. You're not getting me that way!"

He turned and stomped into the house, slamming the door behind him. He knew the doors were locked; unless the door was opened from the inside, the security program would admit only someone who carried the coded pass card. But he checked them anyway, fuming.

He'd made up his mind that he'd have nothing to do with her crazy story, and she'd had him within inches of promising to do whatever she wanted. Like a damn dog, begging for a treat! Well, humans weren't pets, whatever she might think. He almost hoped she'd come back and try again, so he could tell her that.

Right before he told her to go to hell!

CHAPTER 5

IN SCHOOL ON MONDAY JASE looked for Raven, hoping for a chance to say some of the things he'd been rehearsing, but she wasn't there. That night he dreamed that something was searching for him, hunting him. He didn't know what it was, but it frightened him and he hid—even though next morning he couldn't say what "it" had been, or where he'd hidden.

On Tuesday, Jase was so busy trying not to think about Raven that he caught a reprimand from his algebra teacher, and had to stay after school to watch a vid of the lesson. "Since you clearly aren't paying attention to it now."

When he finally escaped the school parking lot was nearly empty, so he saw at once that Raven wasn't waiting by his car either. And there was no reason to feel that surge of disappointment—he didn't *want* to see her again. If she'd found some other human to terrify and seduce and harass, that was fine!

As he walked toward his car, he noticed two Native boys crossing the lot, but there were a lot of school sports going on now. Jase cataloged them as football players leaving practice early . . . until they swerved toward him and grabbed his arms.

"Hey! What's—"

The world spun as they kicked his feet from under him and shoved him face first into the pavement. Sparks of pain flashed from his knees, competing with a throbbing ache that radiated from the cheekbone resting on the asphalt.

Then thought returned. Jase had been punched once or twice by little kids expressing their parents' frustration with *Mintok v. the Native Corp.* Being beaten more seriously, by teenagers, was a fear he'd been suppressing for years.

"It wasn't my fault." His voice sounded fuzzy, even to him. "For God's sake, I was only three!"

He squirmed against the hands that pinned his wrists behind him, but the boys were stronger than he was and had better leverage. If he yelled for help, would the beating part begin? His stomach knotted. But Jase could hear chattering voices, a study group maybe, behind the hedge that screened the courtyard from the parking lot. This was an awfully public place for a beating, and all his attackers were doing right now was . . . going through his pockets?

They were. One held him down while the other pulled his blazer from under him to search, and then ran his hands into Jase's trouser pockets and yanked them inside out. Robbery?

"My credit chip's biolinked," Jase told them. "No one else can use it."

"I don't sense anything," one of them said. "You're sure this is the same car?"

Sense what? What car?

The hands holding Jase's wrists twitched, but no one spoke.

"Yeah? Well you were sure the last three times too," the first speaker continued. "Get him up."

The ground fell away from Jase as they lifted him, with an ease that warned him not to try anything stupid. They shoved him to sit on the Tesla's hood, and then sat down beside him, each holding one of his wrists in a grip that felt more like iron than flesh.

They still looked like high school football players, or at least they were big enough to play. The tall one was thinner, with more aquiline features. The short one wasn't much taller than Jase, but his body was thick with muscle. Linebacker to the other's wide receiver.

Jase knew all the kids at his school, by sight at least, and he was pretty sure he'd never seen them before. The short one looked kind of like the plainclothes cop at the border, only about twenty years younger, which made no sense at all.

"Where is it?" The tall one's voice was coldly impersonal, his indifference emphasized by the pain that throbbed in Jase's cheek. He was going to have a bruise, one that would probably show up even in the security vid. And where was school security? Even if no one was watching the monitors, the computers were set to recognize and alert on anything that even looked like bullying. Which this surely was!

"You know, the school security guards are on their way by now." Jase nodded to the cameras that covered the parking lot. "You should probably go before they get here."

He wouldn't dream of trying to stop them.

The tall one didn't seem to care about the cameras. "Where is it?" he repeated. "Where's the catalyst?"

"The what?" If this wasn't a revenge beating or a robbery, what was it? "I don't know what you're talking about. Are you sure I'm the guy you're looking for?"

The tall one scowled at the short one, who shrugged.

"The medicine pouch," the tall one said. "The one you picked up at the border eleven days ago."

Realization shot through Jase on a blast of adrenaline. But the tall one had given him time to gather his wits.

"I have no idea what you're talking about. I haven't been near any border for five months, and I didn't pick up a pouch or anything. I just drove off the ferry and through customs. And if you're customs agents, I want to talk to your supervisor! And call my father. He's a lawyer," Jase added.

His heart was hammering so hard they could probably feel the pulse in his wrists. Would they buy it? And if they didn't, was he willing to let them beat him up just to keep the pouch away from them? He'd promised Raven, sort of. But she hadn't done anything to earn that much loyalty.

The shapeshifters, Raven's enemies, looked at each other.

"What do you think?" the tall one asked.

The short one's answer was to twist Jase's arm up behind him so hard it felt like his shoulder was coming out of its socket.

"Hey!" Pain made up Jase's mind. "Help! Somebody call security, call the cops, somebody help me!"

He was yelling the final words, but in the silence after he stopped he could hear the voices of the study group on the other side of the bushes. They didn't sound like they'd heard him. Real fear prickled down his spine.

"Help me!" Jase put all the volume, all the fear he could muster into that scream.

The oblivious chatter went on without missing a beat.

The tall one didn't even glance at the hedge. He rose to his feet and pulled a knife out of his pocket, old-fashioned steel, with a five-inch blade that should have set off every security siren in the school the moment the cameras spotted it.

Nothing happened.

Jase threw his weight against the short one's grip, with all his panicked strength. For a moment he thought his shoulder would dislocate, but then his wrist, slippery with sweat, turned in his captor's grip. Jase twisted his arm free and ran.

Looking back would have cost him half a second, and he didn't dare lose even that much speed. He headed straight for the hedge, diving and rolling like an acrobat over any car that blocked his path.

He was shouting for help at the top of his lungs, but it wasn't till he burst through a gap in the bushes and into sight that they finally heard him.

o   o   o

The head of school security didn't believe him.

The bruise on Jase's face wasn't as dark as he'd expected, only faintly blue, and all the kids who'd been working in the courtyard swore they hadn't heard a thing till Jase thrashed through the hedge yelling about cops.

Jase hadn't felt up to explaining alien shapeshifters to his principal—not to mention medicine pouches of contraband. He'd said his assailants were Native teens with a grudge against his father. And that they'd worn hats and had their collars pulled up, so he couldn't identify them.

The head of security promptly offered to bring up security footage of the parking lot during that time period, which gave Jase some bad moments . . . until they found that every security camera fixed on the lot at that time displayed nothing but static.

The principal gave the baffled security chief a look that promised a serious discussion when there were no students around.

The security chief accused Jase of jamming the feed to conceal whatever it was he'd been up to.

Jase said he didn't know enough tech to do that, and that his science teacher would confirm it.

The principal said no one should be able to do that, as the security chief had promised when he recommended that system to the school.

The security chief reminded the principal that no one in the vicinity had heard Jase's *alleged* shouts for help, either.

Maybe, the principal said fairly, the study group was making too much noise to hear anything else. And the hedge could have muffled the shouts, too.

Jase didn't believe it, and that worried him more than the static on the vid. Jamming a security camera was possible, though it took really competent tech. Preventing sound from traveling out of an open-air parking lot was . . . Well, maybe the aliens did have some way to do that. And if Jase's great-great-grandmother could whistle for wind, then maybe it was some sort of magic.

And if they could do that, what else could they do?

This disturbing train of thought derailed when the principal said it was time to call Jase's parents.

He didn't want his parents to know about this. His mother would worry, and that was bad enough. His father would think he'd brought this down on Jase himself. And that guilt would translate to demanding that the police arrest his son's attackers, immediately.

At best, they wouldn't find anyone. At worst they'd arrest a couple of blameless Native kids. And Jase, who'd just sworn that he couldn't possibly identify his assailants, would have to explain why he was so certain those kids weren't guilty.

Jase told the principal that there wasn't much harm done, and he'd rather tell his parents about it himself.

The principal said he'd delay any further action till he heard from Jase's parents regarding their wishes in this matter.

Jase was pretty sure the principal knew he wouldn't be hearing from anyone, but his civilized ass was covered so the matter would be allowed to drop.

He drove home, very late now, with all the car doors locked, looking for football player–sized boys on every block.

When he got home he told his parents he'd fallen on the stairs, but that the school nurse had taken scans and said there was no serious damage. At least that part was true.

He waited till they went to bed before he patrolled the house and checked the locks on every door and window, so he didn't have to explain that either.

o   o   o

Where was Raven? Now Jase wanted to see her, so he could get that pouch out of his garage before something even worse showed up to claim it. She wasn't in school on Wednesday, either. What would he do if she never came back? If even part of what she'd said was true—which now seemed a lot more likely—he couldn't just throw the pouch away. She should have given him her pod code, or whatever it was aliens used to communicate.

The house was more secure than the garage, so Jase moved the pouch into his room and hid it in the back of his desk drawer. Still in its plastic bag, because despite what Georg said, you never really knew. Maybe the airtight bag would keep it from leaking magic as well.

His father told Jase he'd be needed to drive Mr. Hillyard

back to the border on Tuesday, and that he'd clear it with Jase's principal. Which would be fine, if Jase had given the pouch back to Raven by then. If he hadn't . . . As long as Mr. Hillyard was with him he'd be fine. It was the long drive home that worried him.

But there was no reason for football player aliens to be looking for him at the border, Jase told himself firmly. He hadn't seen them again, not at school, or around his home, or anywhere. He'd probably convinced them he didn't have it. The tall one had said he couldn't sense anything, and the short one hadn't been sure they had the right car—which meant that someone must have seen the girl throw the bag over the fence, seen Jase retrieve it, but they hadn't gotten a good look at him or the Tesla. The fact that they couldn't identify his Tesla pretty much proved their alien nature, as far as Jase was concerned. But aliens or not, they didn't seem to be stalking him now.

Unless they were biding their time, waiting till he relaxed his guard.

On Wednesday night Jase dreamed of being hunted again, of hiding, cowering, while something menacing tried to find him. When he woke up enough to think, the dream made sense—being stalked and mugged by aliens who could stop sound was enough to give anyone nightmares. Maybe the principal was right, maybe the study group had been talking too loudly to hear him. Or maybe the aliens had used some advanced sound-damping tech—Jase preferred both those explanations to magic. But he resolved to leave his window clear for a while, anyway. He was getting accustomed to sleeping in the light.

On Thursday he played basketball with Joey and Brendan,

and he was so distracted looking at passing football players, and any girl with long dark hair, that he missed several passes. When he found himself peering into nearby trees for a big black bird, he quit the game and went home early.

Forget it—and they could forget about him, too! If Raven wanted to save the world so bad she could make contact. And if she didn't show up soon, he'd hide the pouch in the woods somewhere and let them all go hunt for it.

When she knocked on his window late Thursday night she woke him out of a sound sleep. About time she showed up!

"Open the window."

Jase could barely hear her through the glass. He hoped his parents couldn't.

"Shh!" He got out of bed and padded over to the window, not bothering to put on his pajama top.

Raven, who'd leaned over the rail to knock on the glass, settled back onto the deck. As Jase drew near enough to look, he saw that this time she was dressed in a man's big flannel shirt . . . and nothing else, as far as he could see. Planning another seduction? He had no intention of falling for it.

"Open the window," she repeated.

Despite his resolution, Jase wished he could. If she was wearing as little as it seemed, watching her climb in would be interesting.

"It doesn't open," he told her. "Go down the deck to the door and I'll let you in."

Moving through the dim hall, Jase was grateful his parents' room was on the other side of the house. But when he reached the big glass door, he still touched a finger to his lips for silence before he pressed the button to slide the door aside.

She'd wrapped her arms around herself, and she stepped

hastily into the warm house. Jase couldn't be sure in the gray twilight, but he thought he saw goose flesh on those long bare legs.

He gestured for silence again, led her back to his room, and closed the door before he spoke.

"Where have you been? I've been waiting for days! Something happened that I need to tell you about."

"Are you carrying the medicine bag?" She sounded as if she hadn't even heard what he said, which annoyed him even more. But in that old-style flannel shirt, with her dark hair falling around her, she looked like the kind of woman who could ask that question. *Good luck on the hunt, my love. Do you have enough ammunition? Your medicine bag?*

Except the way she looked now, any hunter in his right mind would suddenly decide to delay his departure for a few more hours, and—

"Hey!" She waved her hand in front of his eyes, breaking into the beginning of a really nice fantasy. "Where's the pouch? It doesn't seem to be on you, but I can tell it's near."

"If you can tell that, how come he had to turn out my pockets?"

"What? Who's 'he'?"

"A couple of guys, who shook me down in the school parking lot." Jase pulled open the desk drawer, groping till his fingers touched the slick plastic. "They looked like Native kids, about my age. But they didn't fight like kids." He turned his face to the window, showing off the fading bruise. Holistomax had lightened the color, but green and yellow blotches still showed.

"How do you know they were looking for the pouch?"

"Because they asked if I had it—the catalyst, he called it."

Jase held out the pouch, but she just stood there, frowning. "I said I didn't know what they were talking about, because I didn't know anything about a catalyst. Then they told me they were looking for the medicine bag I'd picked up at the border, and I kept saying I didn't know what they were talking about, and one of them pulled a knife on me. I know they were . . . were your people, because after I escaped I started shouting and they stopped the sound. Somehow."

He waited for her to ask how he'd escaped from two high-tech aliens with knives. Which was pretty impressive, when he thought about it.

"When did this happen? Have you seen them since? Do they know where this house is?"

"It was four days ago, and I haven't seen them since. I don't know what they know."

"Hmm. If they followed you they'd have found the house days ago. And if they got close enough they would have sensed the pouch, so they didn't bother to track you down. You must have convinced them you didn't have it." Her expression brightened. "You're a very good liar, Jase Mintok."

"My dad's a lawyer. It's genetic." She evidently didn't care about his courage, determination, and quick wits. "So how come you knew I had this catalyst thing . . . it's the dirt, isn't it? The dust in this bag, it starts something."

"Exactly. Well, not exactly, but close enough."

Jase decided he didn't want to know what it started.

"So how come you can sense it's here, and they didn't know that it wasn't? How come you could find me when they couldn't?"

"I'm more familiar with its energy signature," Raven said. "Though it's changed, since Kelsa abandoned it. And it's about to change again, which should slow them down even more. Hand it over."

Reluctant curiosity stirred once more. "Energy signature?" Jase gave her the medicine bag, and watched her remove its plastic sheath and untie the strings.

"That's the clearest I can say it in your language."

She reached into her pocket and pulled out a bit of folded cloth, then turned on his desk lamp.

"Open this for me, and hold it." She gave the pouch back to Jase as she spoke. "I don't want to drop anything."

Jase held the bag open, trying not to touch its contents. "When you say 'my language,' do you mean English? Or Human?"

"Both." She unfolded the rag, revealing a small pile of what looked like white glitter, speckled with small dead bugs.

"What's that? It's not bugs, is it?" On closer examination, the black bits had neither legs nor wings. In fact they looked like—

"It's rubber." Raven tipped the glittering pile into the medicine bag, then took it from Jase with the delicate firmness of someone handling a baby bird. "I filed it off your car's tires." She stirred the rubber and glitter carefully into the rest of the dust, and smiled. "Oh, good! It's melding."

Jase frowned. That tiny bit of rubber wouldn't hurt his tires, though he'd bet the file left a scar. But the glitter . . .

"You didn't file my *car*, did you?" His voice rose, despite the danger of waking his parents.

"Don't sound so panicked." The imp smile dawned. "It's just a tiny bit off the inside of one of the wheel holes. And a tiny bit off one of the metal parts too, which was hard to file! The tricky part was infusing the whole thing with energy from the batteries," she added. "I had to perform a ceremony for that, and I haven't had to do that kind of beginner exercise to control any form of energy since . . . well, for a very long time. And it took days! But it wasn't like light, or even electricity," she finished thoughtfully. "It was more . . . slippery, I guess."

Jase didn't care how battery energy felt.

"What did you do to my car?"

"Since you wouldn't do this the easy way, I'm using your car, the thing you care about most in the world, to bind you into the medicine pouch's magic."

"You're what?"

She was still smiling, but her dark eyes held a determined glint.

"I also bound your car's essence to the pouch. So if you don't use this magic properly, as it was meant to be used, your car won't work either."

"That's carp. I may have begun to think . . . I mean, maybe those guys did have some cool tech, and maybe some of those old shamans could do stuff. But there's nothing magic about my car. Teslas are the most reliable cars on the road. And besides, there's lots of things, *people,* that I love more."

She considered that. "You probably do love them more, but your car is more a part of *you.* I could have mixed your own blood into this dust"—she tied up the pouch as she spoke—"but that wouldn't have worked, because to you it's only blood. This will matter."

"Carpo," Jase said. "I might be able to believe you could do something to help with the tree plague, but you can't work magic on a machine. They work with steel and physics and . . . and reality."

Though so did sound waves, and the football kids had

messed with them. But that was different, that was part of nature. This was his car.

"You know," said Raven, "I think I liked the old curses better. That trick your computers played, transposing the letters . . . I liked *bullshit* better."

Her eyes were laughing, as they so often did. Flirting with him again?

"Look, I'm giving back your pouch. Maybe, just maybe, you're doing something real with it. But I'm not interested in you, or anything you plan to do. Period."

It wasn't that those two bullies had intimidated him, oh, no. He just wasn't interested.

Who was he trying to kid?

He expected her to call him on it, call him a coward. Then he could get insulted and throw her out.

She met his gaze steadily, all the lurking humor gone. "Not interested. Even if my plan involves the survival of your species?"

"You'll find someone else. Someone who's willing to sleep . . . to help you."

Not that he wasn't willing to sleep with her. It was her using that willingness to manipulate him that he objected to.

"It has to be you," Raven said patiently, "because when she passed you that pouch, Kelsa created a surge of magical potential. She had an incredible talent for healing—it took me months to find her! You don't have that kind of talent, not as far as I can see. But by her sacrifice, Kelsa opened an energy vortex around you. I think it'll give you enough power to finish the job. It had better." Her serious expression shifted into grim. "Because we're running out of time. They found you and dismissed you, and that was an incredible stroke of luck.

They might not look at you again till the healing starts, but we can't count on that. Once we begin opening the ley they'll be able to pick up the changed signature. Then they will be able to track the pouch, and we'll have to move fast to keep you out of their hands."

"I'm sorry." Jase was surprised to realize that he almost meant it. "But I'm not a save-the-world guy. You have the pouch. Go find someone who knows what he's doing. Who believes in it! I wish you luck. Really. But you'll have to find someone else."

Someone who didn't mind being beaten up by football players. It wasn't like he owed her anything—she'd tried to use him, manipulate him. She still was. No, he wanted no part in this, and even if he did, he wasn't what she needed. She needed someone like that girl at the border, someone who really could heal the world with magic.

But Raven didn't look worried. "I knew you'd say that. That's why I also rigged the magic so your car won't run unless you're in it, wearing the pouch. And using the pouch! You'll have about a week to heal the first nexus before it starts to quit, even when you've got the pouch with you."

"You're not listening," Jase said. "I'm not refusing because I'm pissed. Though I am. It's not even because I'm scared, and I'm scared too! I. Can't. Do. It. Which of those words don't you understand?"

"How do you know you can't," Raven asked, "unless you try?"

"All right," said Jase. "I won't do it. Is that precise enough? Take your stupid pouch, and go find someone else to save the world."

"I knew you'd say that too."

Jase was sufficiently irritated that he didn't even try to argue further when she pocketed the pouch and left . . . no matter what she wasn't wearing.

o   o   o

The next morning, his car wouldn't start.

The dash lights lit. The p-ping that accompanied the starter sounded. But when he pressed the reverse button and stepped on the accelerator, the Tesla didn't move.

Cold battery? In late June? He'd been up in the middle of the night—he knew it hadn't been that cold. But nothing else had ever kept the Tesla from starting.

He would *not* believe she could magic his Tesla. But he could believe she'd planted some alien device. Or maybe it was just cold.

Jase turned the car off, got out, and opened the trunk to raise the cover that concealed the battery over the right rear tire. The battery was cool to the touch, but not the freezing cold that could keep the car from starting in midwinter.

On the other hand . . . Jase pressed his palm against the coils of the battery warmer, which was standard issue for any car in Alaska. If battery temp dropped below working level, the charger was supposed to heat the coils as well as charge the battery. Once the car was unplugged and running, it used the batteries' own power, if necessary, to keep them warm. The coils weren't hot, but the temperature in the garage wasn't that cold, either.

Jase went to the passenger seat and punched the button that extruded the diagnostic control panel below the dash. Most car owners never used the diagnostics themselves—some barely knew they existed—but Jase thought he could read them as well as most Tesla mechanics. And any addition to the system that wasn't factory authorized would be flagged in red—which would surely include alien tech! But when he brought up the battery system, every section lit up green on the diagram. So did the motor, and the drive system.

Could the diagnostic system be down too? It was a better explanation than magic.

Jase had to hunt through the menus, but he finally found the manual override to run the battery warmer on command. When he went around and laid his hand on the coils again they were heating nicely, so he went back into the house and made himself a second cup of coffee. With luck he'd be only a little late, and for homeroom that didn't matter.

When he came out and felt the battery, its cover was warm to the touch—easily warm enough to run. Jase closed the panels and made sure the charger had unplugged itself. He turned the security key and pressed the start button. The controls lit, and the familiar p-ping told him the car was ready to roll. He punched reverse, stepped on the accelerator . . . and the car didn't move.

His mother finally drove him to school, over his protests that he'd figure out what was wrong any minute now. He was forty-five minutes late for his first class.

o   o   o

The diagnostics, which should at least have told him what part of the system wasn't functioning, must be broken too. Along with whatever else was broken. Or sabotaged. Because the only other hypothesis was that a girl with midnight hair and warm brown eyes had magicked his car, and he couldn't accept that. Advanced alien technology, that he could believe . . . From a girl who didn't know what golf clubs were?

Jase's mother was meeting a client at the gallery that afternoon, and she'd refused to cancel that to help him tow the Tesla to the shop. If Jase was that impatient, she said, he could call for a tow truck and pay the $120 fee himself. Jase wasn't that impatient. Besides, he knew as much about the Tesla as most mechanics. Certainly enough to spot any alien devices that had been added.

The Tesla was so low to the ground that he had to roll it down the driveway till it straddled the gutter in order to crawl under it, but the neighbors were accustomed to seeing it parked there, with Jase's legs sticking out from under. He liked to maintain the car himself, and should at least be able to figure out what Raven had done.

With the batteries thoroughly warmed, Jase put the car in neutral and pushed the start button. All systems in the diagnostic glowed green as Jase removed the access panels and checked to see if power was flowing from the batteries to the motor—which it wasn't. But the batteries were all fully charged and warm. Could they have done something to the starter's electronics?

Jase was under the car with a tester, tracing the flow of power from the starter to each of the batteries, when the electric motor whirred to life only inches from his nose. He banged his head on the pavement, then dragged himself from under the car. With all the panels open, he could hear the motor's almost-inaudible purr as he stalked around to glare at the girl who leaned against the front fender.

Raven still wore the flannel shirt, but with jeans and gel-soles beneath. The medicine bag was hanging around her neck.

"What did you do? Tamper with the starter's programming?"

One fine brow lifted. "I wouldn't begin to know how to do that. The pouch is here. You're here. That's why it's running."

"Carpo! All the neo-hippie voojoo in the world can't stop an electric motor. It just can't!"

Raven sighed. "You're stubborn, I'll give you that. Go watch what happens to your motor while I walk away."

Jase, who wanted to take a look at the motor anyway, went back to the trunk. Through the clear cover, he could see the inside of the cylinder spin. Then it stopped.

His eyes flashed to Raven, but she was more than fifty feet from the car. Smirking, damn her.

No one else was anywhere near.

Raven walked toward him and the motor began to spin.

She walked away and the motor stopped.

She turned and drew near again, and the motor ran.

She walked away and it stopped.

The next time she came all the way back to where Jase stood, arms folded, scowling.

"You could have tampered with the battery connections. Put in some sort of switch that cuts in and out on a proximity signal."

"Without your finding it? You've looked at every inch of that thing. About four times, by my count."

She was right. He would have found a switch, or any other device embedded in the system.

"You're wearing a damping field then, something that disrupts every kind of energy."

But it was when she walked *away* that the motor stopped.

When she came near, it worked. All the other electronics in the house and the garage were fine. The Tesla's controls lit. The diagnostic computer was live.

Jase's scowl deepened and she laughed.

"Oh, come on. You can admit that I can change into a bird, and my enemies can stop sound, but I can't affect a car?"

Jase looked at the spinning silver cylinder.

"How are you doing this?"

"I convinced your batteries that whenever the pouch isn't nearby they're too cold to run."

"But they're not cold. They're warm."

"They think they're cold."

"Batteries can't think!"

"Yeah, well, they don't know that. Do you want me to walk back and forth some more to prove it?"

Jase looked at the humming motor. She could affect his car. And if she could do that, maybe the rest of it was real. Those football players had been plenty real, and the idea of meeting them again sent cold fear sliding down his spine. But what if the world really was in danger? And he was the only one who could save it? Humanity was clearly doomed. Still . . .

"What is it, exactly, that you want me to do?"

o   o   o

Jase picked her up the next morning, in a Tesla that was running just fine now that he wore the medicine bag under his shirt.

He'd tested it himself after she left. As long as he had the pouch with him, the car ran. When he left the pouch in his room, it didn't. And he'd looked in all the places a proximity switch could have been spliced in, and found nothing.

He'd kept a wary eye out for football players and not seen a sign of them. He must have convinced them he knew nothing. According to Raven, they'd keep looking elsewhere till he healed the ley. With magic. So he'd probably never see them again. Given the choice between fighting football players and losing his car, well, sometimes you had to take a risk.

That evening at dinner he told his parents he'd be out with friends all day Saturday. If his father didn't have a job for him, Jase often spent weekends hanging with Ferd or Mick or Brendan—they didn't question it.

Raven was waiting on the curb just before he reached the ramp onto Highway 1. The sun was shining today, and she was wearing a stretchie and using the flannel shirt as a jacket. The stretchie wasn't as tight as the top she'd worn to seduce him, but Jase noticed that several cars slowed as they passed.

He still couldn't forgive her for hexing his car, but he felt a twinge of pride that a girl who looked like that was waiting for him.

He'd left the top down, and she climbed nimbly over the low door.

"Where are we going?" Jase headed for the highway, since he was pretty sure whatever was going to take place would be a nature thing, not a middle-of-Anchorage thing. And the sooner they were finished, the sooner his car would be free. If he tried his best and failed, surely she'd be willing to let his car go before she went to find someone else.

"That way." She pointed east. "We want trees for this."

On the highway the wind was too loud to converse in anything softer than a shout, so they said very little.

Somewhat to Jase's surprise, Raven told him not to turn off on Highway 3, which led north to Denali and Fairbanks, but he didn't mind. Past Palmer, away from the cameras and speed recorders of the grid, the traffic thinned. Eventually, Jase came across a long straight stretch with no traffic at all and let the Tesla go.

Some girls squealed when he punched the accelerator and the g-force threw them back against their seat. With the top up, it felt like riding a roller coaster. With the top down, Jase thought, it felt more like being fired out of a cannon.

Raven threw back her head and laughed. Her hair writhed in the backwash, the tips flicking Jase's face and neck till she gathered it up with both hands and twisted it into a thick coil.

Treacherous as she'd proved herself to be, Jase found the idea of getting his hands into that silky hair so distracting that he had to slow down, because he wasn't paying enough attention to the road.

"Wow!" Raven shouted as the wind died back to its normal rush. "I didn't know you could go that fast, in this form."

That was such a startling idea that Jase took his foot off the accelerator, and the car slowed sharply.

"Is that what it's like to fly?"

"Yes. No. In a way. The sense of speed can be like that, particularly when you're diving. But this car, it's completely rooted to the earth. Flying is all about air. And sometimes you have to put a lot of effort into flying, and then it's nothing like—oh, we've arrived. Pull off here."

Jase had expected . . . he didn't know what he'd expected, but it wasn't an ordinary pullout in the middle of the taiga.

"I know they look sick," Jase said, "but the tree plague hasn't reached here yet. The icky woods always look like this."

Scraggly and misshapen, the treetops drooping wearily, this had to be the least beautiful forest in the world. One of his mother's European friends had said that she'd never been to Chernobyl, but now she knew what it would look like. It was one of his first-grade classmates who'd dubbed them "the icky woods," and for Jase the name had stuck.

"I know the plague isn't here yet," said Raven. "The leys where it's set in are so poisoned that it's going to take more than one human to heal them. What we're doing here is strengthening this ley so it can't spread north. Once we've healed the leys that ring the plague, stopped it from spreading, we can work inward and heal the disease itself."

"Leys plural?" Jase asked. "We? All of them? I want my car back!"

"Not you," Raven assured him. "Other humans can do the rest. I told you, if we can heal one ley, open all its nexuses so the power flows strong and clean, the neutrals will keep my enemies in check so I can do the rest. Kelsa opened this ley from the central crossing all the way to Alaska. Now the power's building at a . . . sluggish point, right here. If you can free it, I think healing just two more points would leave it clear all the way to the terminal node."

"So if I can just do three of these healing things, the football players will leave me alone?"

"Forever. I have the neutrals' word on that."

She seemed to trust that a lot more than Jase did. And once the Tesla was running again, all these neutrals and enemies would be none of his business.

"All right then." Jase got out of the car and went around to help her. "What do I do?"

Somewhat to his annoyance, Raven wiggled out of the low seat without his help.

"First we have to hike a little way into the woods. You need to be able to touch the trees, and I'm afraid the traffic would distract you."

Jase had thought they might go hiking—New-Agey nature healing—so he'd worn waterproof boots, and put a pack with water and trail snacks into the trunk.

"Let me get the car locked up." A few pushed buttons later the Tesla was protected from both thieves and rain, and Jase was once more tramping into the wilderness on Raven's heels.

They hadn't walked for more than ten minutes before she stopped, and looked around at the damp, mossy woodland.

"We're right on top of a nexus here, and the taiga—your "icky woods"—appears all over central Alaska. If you can reach it, heal the ley through these trees and plants, power should be able to flow all the way to the node once a couple of places on the coast have been opened."

"You said these trees weren't sick." A mosquito buzzed near, drawn by the warmth of his body, and he swatted at it. His repel-vacs were up-to-date, but sometimes Alaskan mosquitoes didn't care. "Why do we have to heal them if the tree plague isn't here?"

Raven looked impatient, but her voice was serious when she replied, "It's not so much that you're healing the trees, it's that in joining them to the power of the ley you'll be freeing their power. The type of nature that you heal here will help to clean and invigorate the leys wherever they connect. This kind of vegetation, the sparse taiga, reaches all through the north of this continent and into Siberia. If you can heal this ley through the taiga, I'll have a head start on more major leys as well."

This made no sense to Jase—but he hadn't expected it to

make sense. The sooner he tried, the sooner she'd release his car. "OK. What do you want me to do?"

Raven sighed. "First, sit down."

She settled onto one of the mossy tussocks, and Jase eyed the one behind him dubiously. The seat of his pants wasn't waterproof. He touched the moss, finding it soft and not too wet, so he seated himself facing the girl.

"Now what?"

"You have to . . . open communication between yourself and the trees, the moss, all the living plants around us. Once you've—"

"Wait, communicate? You want me to talk to the trees?"

"Not just the trees, though they'd do. And not just talk. You need to—"

"You brought me here to talk to a tree?" Though given what he'd seen her do, maybe that wasn't as crazy as it sounded. "Will it talk back?"

Raven rubbed her temples, as if they were beginning to ache.

"When I say 'communicate,' I don't mean talk like we're doing. You need to open yourself, your energy, and connect it to theirs. Once you've established a connection, your intent can affect that shared energy. You'll probably need to use an incantation to focus it; most humans do. When you're connected and focused, then you scatter a pinch of the catalyst. The catalyst will seal and amplify the connection, so your will to heal can become reality."

Jase looked around dubiously. Dark scrawny spruce trees. Little bushy things. Yellow-brown moss and swamp mud, because the taiga was a swamp.

"Open myself how? Stop scowling like that. I'm willing to try, but I just don't get it!"

She did her best to explain, and he continued to try for the next two hours, but he never got it. He'd never been more glad to get into the car and drive a girl home in his life. And at least his abysmal failure as a magical healer meant that he didn't have to search the shadows around his garage for lurking football players. But it still felt like failure.

"I told you to find someone else," he said. He wouldn't mind at all, as long as she let his car go before she vanished.

"No," said Raven. "I think I tried to start you out too fast. Baby steps, that's what we need. And for you to be less frustrated."

"I have a feeling I'm going to be frustrated for a long time," Jase said gloomily, and didn't even think about the double meaning till Raven laughed.

She said she'd come and get him first thing tomorrow, to start whatever "baby steps" she had in mind. When Jase got home, he told his parents he'd be gone the next day and went to bed still frustrated by his failure. And in other ways as well.

He was ready to hide at the first flicker of the shadow, but instead someone knocked on the inside of his closet door.

"Who's there?"

It wasn't exactly an invitation, but he wasn't surprised when the old woman stepped out of his closet.

"The energy of the catalyst has changed. It's so corrupted I can't find it at all. But you're closer to it, aren't you?"

The pouch was back in his desk drawer, which Jase supposed was closer than the garage—but he wasn't about to tell her that.

TRAITOR'S SON · 101

"I have no idea what you're talking about," he said. It had worked on the football players, after all. "And I think you're the one who sent . . . something to hunt me, didn't you? In my dreams? Well, I want it to stop. Call it off, whatever it is."

She stood perfectly still in the center of his room, but her expression put Jase in mind of one of his grandfather's dogs, sniffing scents on the wind.

"Yes, you're bound into it now. I can sense that much, at least. He found you."

"That boy you told me about? I haven't seen him."

The dark old eyes were fierce. "You're ly—oh. Of course he'd change. You're not a liar, boy. You're an idiot."

"Thanks," said Jase. "I have no idea what you're talking about, and I don't—"

"That's why you're an idiot," the old woman said. "But you don't have to die for it. Tell me where you are, where the pouch is. I'll come get it, and you'll see no more of any of us. In dreams or out of them."

Realization dawned. This wasn't just a dream. "You're a shapeshifter! You're . . ."

One of Raven's enemies.

"Oh, yes," she said. Jase prayed she was reading his expression, instead of his mind. "But Raven's no more your friend than I am—though I've no doubt she's prettier. Did she tell you what happened to the last human she talked into carrying that dust?"

"The girl who threw it over the border fence? Raven said she'd been arrested, though she was released later."

"She was arrested. And it saved her life. Because if she hadn't thrown herself into the custody of human guards, *she'd have been killed by our ambush just four miles past the border. Yes, we'd have killed her for the dust she carried. And if you use it, we'll kill you too. Spare yourself, boy. Spare your parents that grief. Tell me where you are, and let me take that pouch off your hands."*

No one had ever threatened to kill him before, not someone who meant it. The memory of his face slamming into the asphalt parking lot returned, vividly, and his cheekbone throbbed again. Jase clasped his hands around his knees to hide the fact that they wanted to shake.

"If you're willing to kill me, I'd really be an idiot to tell you where I am. Besides, Raven says that if the leys aren't healed the tree plague will spread through the world and everyone will die."

And if he gave away that pouch, his car might never run again.

The old woman snorted. "What nonsense! Do you really think the world could be destroyed by a few sick trees?"

"It was almost destroyed by a few degrees' change in temperature," Jase said. "Not that long ago. I've taken biology. This planet's atmosphere, its oxygen, comes from the forests. They say the tree plague won't spread out of the Tropics, but if it did we'd be in real trouble!"

"But your own scientists say it won't spread far," the old woman pointed out. "Why not trust them?"

"I might trust them," Jase said. "I don't trust you. Get out of my room."

Or did he mean out of his dream? In either case, he was going to do something about it.

Jase had given up on golf years ago, but the putter his father had told him to practice with was still stuck behind *his dresser. Jase got it and stood before the old woman. She was shorter than he was, and had to be much weaker, but she didn't look frightened.*

"Go," said Jase. "I'll use it. I swear I will."

"You think that can hurt me? You're dreaming."

He was dreaming, wasn't he? It wasn't as if she was a real person, who might actually be injured. So Jase swung the putter with all his might, and almost fell over when it passed right through her.

The old woman smiled. "Your weapons have no power here. Mine, on the other hand . . ."

She stepped forward and slapped him, hard enough to rock his head to one side, hard enough that Jase woke up, standing in the middle of the room with his heart pounding.

The closet door was closed. The old woman was gone. But his face still stung from the force of her slap.

CHAPTER 6

JASE SLEPT IN NEXT MORNING, and woke up still debating whether or not to tell Raven about his dreams. On one hand, that old lady was one of her enemies. On the other hand . . .

I had a terrible nightmare—a little old lady slapped me. It wasn't the kind of thing he wanted to say to an attractive girl. And the old woman hadn't found him. And the football players were convinced that he didn't have the pouch.

And after all, they were only dreams.

He still hadn't made up his mind when he went downstairs and found Raven talking to his parents.

"What are . . . Ah, I see you've all met."

"I said first thing this morning," Raven reminded him. "It's almost nine. But your parents were kind enough to offer me breakfast."

"We like meeting Jase's friends," his mother told her.

"Even if they're still in the 'haven't made up my mind what to do with myself' club," his father added. "Of which Jase is a charter member."

But the look he gave Jase had less to do with criticism and more to do with *wow!*

His father was in love with his mother, and Jase knew he'd

never look seriously at a girl Raven's age. But a man would have to be dead not to appreciate her.

How dare she introduce herself to his parents, without asking him first?

"Let me grab a heat-go sandwich, and we'll get out of here," Jase said.

"Great. Your mother was kind enough to pack lunch for us."

Raven and his mother exchanged a look he couldn't read, but he didn't think it meant *wow.*

"Raven tells us she's going to teach you to appreciate nature," his mother said. "I warned her it was likely to be an uphill fight—you're worse than your father! But I certainly wish her luck."

Was "let's start to change the guy right now" a female version of *wow?* Jase doubted it.

"I won't give up," Raven promised. "Not if it kills both of us."

His parents laughed.

Jase knew better.

o   o   o

"You should have asked me, before you showed yourself to my parents." Jase pulled the Tesla out of the driveway.

"If I'd asked, what would you have said?"

"No! I don't want my parents involved in this."

"That's why I didn't ask. It was interesting to meet your parents."

Jase turned onto the street. He didn't want to discuss his family.

"Where to?" he asked. "We've already been to the most boring part of the state. How about doing dangerous next? Spelunking in glacier crevasses, maybe?"

Raven grinned. "You're going to learn to appreciate nature, just like I told your mother."

Jase snorted.

"Seriously. Nature is part of everyone's heritage. Maybe you should get closer to yours."

"That's what my grandfather says. I attribute every bee sting and sprained ankle I ever had to my heritage."

She laughed. "Then let's start with something safer. The Ananut are matrilineal, right? What's your mother's mother's last name?"

"Harrigan," Jase said dryly.

"You think the Irish don't appreciate nature?"

"I'll have to turn at the stop sign," Jase pointed out. "It would be nice to know where I'm going."

"All right." Her expression shifted into serious. "Is there someplace, anyplace at all, where you feel at peace in nature? Someplace that makes your soul feel open and still."

Jase started to frame a crack about nightclubs, and the wildlife therein, but something in her face stopped him. The sooner she gave up on him, the sooner he'd get his car back.

"There's . . . I've been to Potter Marsh on school field trips. It's OK."

He actually thought it was beautiful, but surrounded by the spectacular scenery of Alaska, he feared that small, home-made marsh would seem pretty tame.

"It's quiet," he added. "Even with tourists around. And they'll be there, on a Sunday."

"That's where we're going," Raven said firmly. "Potter Marsh."

On Sunday most of the traffic was headed into the city, but

Potter Marsh was so close to Anchorage that it hardly mattered. Maybe afterward they could go appreciate nature farther down the road to the south. There was plenty of nature there, but also some nice restaurants and clubs. The Kenai Peninsula was Anchorage's wilderness playground.

Potter Marsh ran beside the road, but the turnoff to the parking lot came before you could see it. Jase pulled the Tesla out of the traffic, and within moments he had Raven on the boardwalk and through the trees, and the marsh spread out before them.

It was kind of lame, Jase supposed. But a cool breeze stirred the long grass, turning it from green to silver in sweeping waves. The dark water, as they stepped along the walkway above it, was full of salmon fry, from big-trout size to toothpick. Yellow butterflies perched on the deck when they weren't in flight.

"This wasn't here before." Raven stared at the marsh in astonishment.

"Before what? It was created when they built the railroad," Jase told her. "They changed the grade or something and ended up with this really big puddle, and decided to turn it into a wetland instead of draining it. So it's almost two centuries old. But . . . the quiet's so loud, you can hear it over the highway noise."

He felt stupid the moment he said it, but she nodded. "You're right. Now go on. Tell me what you see here. What makes this place what it is."

A Canada goose with a flotilla of goslings paddled by as Jase talked. A swallow, perched on a rail, let the tourists with their flashing com pods get amazingly close before it flew.

"And those yellow lilies," Jase finished. "They grow in

ponds all over Alaska. They look like they'd smell sweet, but I got close to one once when my grandfather made . . . took me fishing. They don't have any scent, except maybe a bit resiny. And the one I grabbed was full of ants."

"Then there's something sweet about them," Raven said, "whether you can sense it or not. But you're right about this place—you can feel the life in it. You can, can't you?"

Jase could, though he'd never put it into words before. He nodded.

"Then it's time to go back," she said. "And give the taiga another try."

o   o   o

"I was hoping we could go south today," Jase grumbled as they drove back down Highway 1. Between the chill of the breeze and the clouds scudding across the sky, he'd decided to keep the top up. "Or maybe turn north this time, toward Denali. Denali's got lots of nature—trees and things." And there were good restaurants there as well, catering to the tourists. "Couldn't we do this healing thing in Denali?"

Raven sighed. "You should be glad you've got me to walk you through this. Remember me talking about the ley's terminal node? The place where all its power spirals in, and is cleaned and amplified?"

Jase frowned. "Denali's the terminal node? Then why don't we just do the healing thing there? If it's that big and important, maybe we wouldn't have to do the smaller places."

He was looking at the road then, but he could feel Raven wince.

"If you *could* connect with the ley at Denali, and dropped the catalyst there, one of two things would probably happen.

The first is that it would simply ignore you, and not react at all."

"Then why don't we—"

"The second," said Raven grimly, "is that every volcano on the Pacific Rim would erupt. Or something equally devastating. When you clear a nexus you release a lot of power. Igniting a node . . ." She shuddered.

"OK, no nodes," Jase said. "You're the expert."

"Remember that," said Raven. "But you can't tell me you don't sense . . . Did you really think Denali was just a mountain? Or Niagara just a waterfall?"

"I've never seen Niagara Falls," Jase said. "Though Mother says it's spectacular. But Denali's the tallest mountain in North America. And it starts just a few hundred feet above sea level, so that's even more impressive. It's so high it makes its own weather, which is why you hardly ever see the peaks. It—"

"Those are facts," said Raven. "What's the truth? What does your soul know about Denali?"

Jase thought about it. Then he tried to find the words, and to his own surprise they came.

"Denali is like thunder."

"Well," said Raven. "At least you're not totally deaf."

They seemed to reach the pullout more quickly today. The top was already up, and within moments Jase was following Raven through the trees. At least the icky woods cut the wind, so he wasn't shivering when they reached the same drab grove where he'd failed so abysmally the last time.

"Couldn't we try this somewhere else?" he asked. "Like, a fresh start. Wouldn't that help?"

"No," said Raven. "I need to prove to you that you can do this, so you'll know how to do it anywhere on the ley. The next place I want you to heal is the sea along the south coast. How will you do that if you don't know that you can reach out to the ley through all living nature, not just the things you're comfortable with?"

"I get seasick," Jase said. "What's the last ley? The inside of a live volcano?"

"It's not the last ley," said Raven. "It's the last natural system on the ley, and it's air. You could probably do that almost anywhere near the ley, since air is so fluid. But reaching it will be harder for you than connecting with something you can see and touch, so regard this as an exercise. Sit down, and look at this place with the same eyes you used in Potter Marsh. Listen with the ears that heard Denali's thunder. And tell me about *this* place."

Brown moss and icky trees.

"But this is a swamp!"

"And the difference between a swamp and a wetland is?"

"A wetland is full of life," Jase said. "This is all . . ."

He looked at a nearby black spruce. Now that he was examining it up close, it was still scrawny and scraggly, but the fat green fingers of needles on the few branches it had didn't look stressed or . . . unhappy.

"No salmon fry here." Jase went to the edge of a boggy patch to check, and there were no salmon fry—but the water was clear as crystal over the muddy bottom. Glossy black dragonflies, and a few iridescent blue ones, buzzed over the pond. He heard the chirp and twitter of songbirds, and the booming toy-horn honk of a tree frog.

Jase sat on a thick clump of moss, and for the first time in his life *looked* at the moss around him. It was brown, but it wasn't dead. Its feathery fronds, soft under his fingers, had a golden undertone. And it didn't choke out the other plants. He saw dozens of different leafy things, and the whole moss bed was studded with flowers, white and yellow, and tiny, fragile pink ones.

"I thought this was a sickly place." His voice was soft with astonishment. "I mean, stuck down in the bog and all. But it's so . . . alive."

"Bogs are full of life. The taiga is one of the strangest, harshest ecosystems in the world. The reason it's so wet is because it rests on solid ice—water can't seep away. And it has to burn before it can grow. Black spruce seeds won't germinate without fire. That damp moss you're sitting on is incredibly flammable."

The tree frog honked again, and Jase let that subtle, fragile sense of life seep into him, just like dampness from the bog beside him seeped into the moss.

"It hums," he said. "Like the motor in my car."

Raven rolled her eyes. "What is it with guys and cars? No, don't answer that. Focus on that hum, how alive, how right it feels. Now, take a pinch of dust, cast it over the taiga, and say the words that will spark its healing."

"But it's not sick." He knew that now, bone deep.

"Not here," said Raven. "But in other places it is. And if you can do this, all those damaged places can be made well, like this one."

That sounded good to Jase. He held on to the awareness of life around him as he untied the knot and opened the pouch. His car was in this dust, somehow. An unknown man, someone that Kelsa girl had cared about, was here. And so was the magic of a shaman, who had died two hundred years ago so that Jase could do this.

"What are the words?" he asked. "What do I say?"

"It's your magic," said Raven. "Say what's in your heart."

Jase looked over the taiga. It wasn't ugly anymore.

"Carp, I hope this works."

He scattered a generous pinch of the dust over the bog, the moss, and the nearest tree.

For a moment it felt like everything around him held its breath. Then the tree branches thrashed and the leafy things rustled as if a great wind had swept over them, though there was no wind.

The surge of power that slammed through Jase a second later was so strong it knocked him off the tussock and into the bog.

The top few inches of water were warm from the intermittent sun; the rest felt as cold as the ice beneath it.

"Carp!" Jase floundered back onto dry land and looked down at the mud on his soaked clothing and boots. Then he looked at Raven, who was lying on her side screaming with laughter.

He was too happy to care. "Hey! That worked, didn't it? I did magic!"

"So you did." Her voice was still unsteady, but she pulled herself together and sat up, hands clasped around her knees. "Your incantation was a bit . . . original, but it worked! Which is all that matters. Come on, let's get you back to the car before you freeze."

∘ ∘ ∘

It would be late evening by the time they got back to Anchorage, but after he'd exchanged his wet clothes for dry rain gear, and the car's heater had kicked in, Jase didn't care.

"I did it! I did magic! Myself!"

"Yes." Raven sounded more serious than Jase thought the situation called for. "But the bad news is that my enemies will have felt the change in the ley as clearly as you and I did. Which means we have to do the next two healings before they can find you. Could you not go to school tomorrow?"

"If I have to," Jase said. "But it took you a week to find me in the first place, and you knew what the pouch felt like. Don't we have a few days? You said we're doing the seacoast next? I'll be driving one of Dad's clients back to the border on Tuesday, and we could drop down to Valdez after."

The football players were scary, but they hadn't struck him as the best and brightest. Remembering the old woman's furious face, they might be the lesser evil. But she was just a dream. And she'd never gotten his address. It was that burning contempt that made her so terrifying.

"Do the rest of your people really hate us so much they'd damage their own world just to destroy us?" Jase asked. "Wouldn't letting us heal the leys make a lot more sense?"

"That's what I keep saying," Raven told him. "And Frog People and Goose Woman agree with me. If we can heal just this one ley, the neutrals will come over to our side. Some of them, anyway. The neutrals are the ones who set the rules for this fight. Including that we all have to use the things of this world, human tools, human magic, to accomplish our goals.

"Which is why a human has to do the healing," she went on. "But it's also why they can't just waltz in and kill you themselves."

"They can't kill me? Nobody told the football player with the knife that!"

"He wouldn't have killed you," Raven said. "They bent the

rules just by threatening you, directly, because they aren't allowed to take the pouch from you by force or magic. They were trying to trick you into handing it over, and thank goodness you were too smart to fall for it!"

A warm glow started in Jase's heart.

"Unfortunately," Raven went on, "they're a lot more adept at using human tools than I thought they'd be. Are you sure you can't get out of school tomorrow?"

"How long do you think it will take them to find the pouch now?" Jase asked. "Seriously."

She hesitated. "I honestly don't know. They've already found you once. It really depends on how you . . . smelled to them, for want of a better word, and how well that matches the scent of you now in the energy signature."

"They weren't sniffing me." But he knew she meant something other than scent, and went on quickly, "I was panicking then. I probably feel pretty different now. Can't we wait just one day? The principal OKs those things, as long as I review vids of all the classes I miss. I could meet you in Valdez Tuesday evening and make it home late Wednesday night. As long as I'm in school Thursday, my parents won't care."

And if they should happen to sign on to Travelnet and check the GPS log of the car's movements, Jase would tell them he'd planned to pay a quick visit to his grandparents and then changed his mind. They wouldn't hold that against him.

And speaking of holding grudges . . .

"I forgive you," said Jase, "for hexing my car. And . . ."

His face was hot.

"I can't unhex it," Raven told him. "The only way to get your car back is to heal the ley."

"I'm OK with that, now. So we can wait for a day?"

"Probably." She sounded pretty reluctant.

But if the football players weren't allowed to beat him up, and the old woman hadn't even found him, how much could one more day hurt? If he ditched school, his father wouldn't let him drive Mr. Hillyard back to the border. If he stopped being a reliable driver, the firm would stop hiring him—and technically, the Tesla still belonged to them.

"You can meet me in the parking lot after school," Jase said. "And protect me from the bad guys. I still don't get why they won't leave us alone to heal stuff. That's what they want in the end, anyway!"

Raven sighed. "They say that the more your technology advances, the more power you have to destroy. That even if you made some progress lately, eventually you'll do something so terrible we won't be able to bring the leys back. So it's better to stop you now. That once you're gone, we can come in and heal the leys ourselves, and this time they'll stay clean."

"Like"—Jase groped for an analogy—"like a grain silo infested with rats. You might bring in an exterminator, poison them all, even though the grain in the silo will have to be discarded. Sacrificing one harvest, so the grain stored there in the future will be all right."

"Exactly," Raven said. "And you can't say human farmers wouldn't make that choice."

They probably had. Jase didn't know much about grain silos.

"But we aren't rats."

When she'd said "human tools," Jase had assumed she meant "tools humans use." Now he wasn't so sure.

Was Raven using a human tool too? Yet surely this afternoon, there'd been admiration as well as laughter in her eyes. Jade decided, again, not to tell her about his dreams.

That night, when the old woman stepped out of Jase's closet, he almost expected it.

"You should close the door behind you," he said. "It's rude, leaving it open like that."

And he didn't like the idea of an open portal to wherever she came from in his bedroom. Maybe he should put a lock on his closet door. Would that stop her?

"I warned you, boy."

"Yeah, but since your plan is to kill all the rats, I don't think I've got much to lose."

The cold anger in her expression was more intimidating than if she'd raved at him. Again, she reminded Jase of his grandfather.

"Rats?" she asked.

"Never mind."

If she didn't already think of humanity as expendable vermin, he'd rather not move her thoughts in that direction. Besides, the wisps of darkness swirling in the closet behind her worried Jase more.

"What's that?"

She smiled. It wasn't reassuring.

"Your people called it Olmaat. Others have called it other things."

"The monster in the woods, who eats people?"

"Near enough."

The wisps of black mist were coalescing.

"But the Olmaat's just an Ananut version of the bogeyman. A scary story, made up to frighten children."

Her smile widened, and for some reason that was terrifying. "You think the Boggle Man wasn't real?"

The darkness in his closet thickened, hardened, as if about to take shape.

"I want to wake up now," Jase said firmly.

The old woman laughed.

Two long sooty tentacles flowed out of the closet. As they passed her, the faces of otters formed on their tips.

Jase had always thought of otters as cute and friendly. He'd never seen them snarl. Or realized how sharp their teeth were, until one of the heads snapped at him.

Jase flinched back, but it came so close, its whiskers brushed his shoulder, and he felt the warmth of its breath on his chilled skin.

He yelped and rolled out of bed, leaping for the bedroom door. The others' bodies might be formless darkness, but those teeth looked real. The old woman's slap had hurt. If this thing caught him . . .

He slammed the bedroom door behind him and ran for his parents' room—long past caring about how stupid he looked running from a dream. But as he ran, the forest grew out of the walls beside him, and the carpet turned to dirt and pine needles under his feet. He was lost before he'd taken a dozen strides.

"Wake up, wake up," he chanted under his breath. But his mind didn't oblige him.

The woods were all too real, stones and broken branches bruising the soles of his bare feet. It had rained here, recently. Cold droplets fell from the branches he shoved aside, and through the fresh scent of rain he could smell the thing behind him; dead fish, dead flesh, and something acrid like the stench of burning plastic.

Jase tripped and fell to his knees. One felt like it hit a rock, and pain lanced up his leg, but he didn't dare stop. The thrashing sound of something pushing through the trees behind him was getting louder.

He flung himself through the next grove and almost ran into a rock wall before he saw it. Were they changing the terrain, trying to trap him?

Jase scrambled along the base of the rocky abutment—it was about forty feet high, and far too steep to climb. The uneven ground at its base, studded with boulders, slowed him down, but Jase followed the wall. If he could find a place to climb up, maybe it would put him out of the thing's reach. Maybe.

"Wake up, wake up!"

The problem was, Jase was no longer certain he was dreaming. His breath rasped in his lungs, and blood had glued the fabric of his pajamas to his skinned knee. He didn't dare to disbelieve.

Running away wasn't working. He needed a weapon.

Jase started to search for one as he ran. A thick branch, or even a rock. But all the large branches he saw were attached to trees, and all the rocks large enough to use were too big to lift.

He tried once more to wake up, to get back to the world where his real body slept, and felt bed sheets slide over his skin, and a distant jolt, as if he'd fallen out of bed.

He tried to move that body, back in the real world, down the hall to his parents' room—surely they could wake him.

But while he concentrated on his sleeping body the cliff beside him vanished, leaving him in a maze of trees, and the monster gained on him as he thrashed his way back to the relatively clear space near the rock wall. If it took him in the trees, he wouldn't stand a chance.

He didn't stand a chance no matter where it took him, unless he could find something to use as a weapon!

Jase started grabbing the larger branches as he ran past trees, trying to break one off, but the only branches that broke were too flimsy to use as a club.

He was so busy searching for a weapon that he almost missed the narrow gap in the rock, but a faint gleam from deep in the crevice caught his eye, and he stumbled to a stop and turned back to look.

He couldn't see much in the dim light, but the cavern went back a little way, and the opening was so narrow he could barely squeeze through. It might stop the monster. And even if it didn't, he couldn't run forever.

Jase wiggled into the cave more by touch than by sight, moving so fast it left bruises on his back and hips. After the first few feet, it widened into a space that might be the size of a closet, though the ceiling was lower.

The glow that had lured him in came from a spear, thrust tip down into the floor and shimmering with pale blue light.

Jase wrapped his hands around the smooth wooden shaft and pulled. Only after it was in his hands did Excalibur *and* hope I'm worthy *flash through his mind.*

Either he was worthy, or the rules were different for spears.

Rock scraped and cracked outside the cave's entrance,

and the husky grunts of the monster's breath were audible even over the sound of his own gasping.

The spear still glowed, giving just enough light for Jase to see a long, otter-faced arm questing into the cave. Its eyes narrowed when it saw him, and it emitted a snarling hiss. Then it darted right at him.

Jase gripped the spear and sliced at it. He missed by several inches, but the face, on its long snaky neck, zigged up to avoid the point and rapped itself on the low ceiling.

It squeaked and blinked rapidly.

Jase's giggle was half hysteria and half sheer terror, but the fact that the thing could be hurt steadied him.

The otter face glared and lunged again. This time Jase thrust the spear, not at the weaving head, but at the thick furry arm that was pinned in place by the narrow crevice of the entrance.

The spear sank into flesh, maybe three inches deep.

The monster's furious roar shattered bits of rock off the ceiling, shattered the darkness, shattered the world.

Jase woke up, sitting in the Tesla, in the dark garage in his own home. Arctic twilight glowed through the windows. Plenty of light. Glorious light. He would never opaque his windows again.

His hands were wrapped around the steering wheel so tightly his knuckles were white. One of his knees was bleeding.

CHAPTER 7

"Jehoshaphat!" Raven stared at him in astonishment. "You're a dreamer."

Jase might be stupid, but he wasn't that stupid. The first thing he'd done, when he came out of school that afternoon and found Raven waiting by his car, was tell her all about his dreams.

"What does that mean?"

He'd been trying all day to convince himself that he'd picked up the ragged gash on his knee and the bruises on his body sleepwalking down to the garage—but he didn't believe it. That dream had been too real, too painful, to be only a dream.

"It wasn't just a dream," he added. "Was it?" He wished with all his heart that she'd say yes.

"Yes," said Raven. "But there are different kinds of dreams. This is the part where you really should have paid attention when your grandfather talked about your heritage. You say he's a shaman. I wonder if the spirit walks too. It can run in families."

"Spirit walking." Jase might not have paid attention to his grandfather, but his social studies teacher had done a whole semester on Alaska Native history and traditions two years ago.

"You mean the kind of dreams a shaman has, when he walks in the spirit world?"

"Exactly. But what they call the Spirit World is what one of your scientists might call an interdimensional interface."

"So"—Jase groped for some middle ground between Native spirituality and physics—"so when I'm dreaming, I'm in your world? Your dimension?"

"Not in it," said Raven. "Your body is, apparently, running around your house tripping on things. And it sounds like you have some sense of it. I've heard that human dream walkers could do that, split their consciousness. But while most of your body is in this world, your mind, and at least some part of your physicality, is manifesting in the Spirit World. And it's not 'my dimension,'" she added. "That's not possible for humans. I'm talking about a . . . a between place, where our two realities overlap."

"How come I can't exist in your dimension and you can exist in mine?"

"It's because we're shifters," Raven told him. "We can materialize bodies pretty much anywhere our consciousness can go. As much of them, or as little, as we want. When your club went—"

"It was a putter."

"Whatever it was, it went right through Otter Woman, and then she manifested enough to slap you. That took some very deft manipulation on her part, but there's no reason she couldn't do it again, and her allies can do it too. This spirit walking, with the enemies you have, it's really dangerous."

"Gee." Jase cupped one hand around his bandaged knee. The damage was invisible under his jeans, but it still throbbed. "Just because they can hurt me and I can't even touch them, you think that's . . . Hey, what about the Olmaat? I hurt him with my spear. I know I did! Is he different from the others?"

"He is different," said Raven slowly. "But that's not why you could hurt him. I think that spear is something from your world that you brought into the Spirit World with you."

"I've never seen that spear before in my life," Jase said. Even if it had been in some museum showcase, the spear had a polished, elegant deadliness he couldn't have forgotten.

"Oh, it's not a spear in this world," said Raven. "It's something else, which your dreaming mind shaped into a weapon—probably because you needed one so badly."

"How could I do that? Could I do it with other weapons?"

Jase had never been a gun person, but a pistol would have been very useful in that cave. And if it was a dream weapon, he should be able to reset the DNA trigger lock so he could fire it.

"No, you can't," said Raven, crushing his dawning hope that he'd found a way to defend himself. "I'm afraid I'm the one who made that spear possible."

"You made the spear? How did you know I'd need it?"

"It's not a spear," she repeated. "Not here. Think a minute. It's something that could follow you into the Spirit World. It has to be bound to you on many levels—magically, almost a part of you. A thing that has some aspect that isn't entirely of this dimension. And it's something you had to run through the woods and crawl into a cave to reach."

"I get it." Jase gazed wonderingly at his car's control panel. "I got it as soon as you said it had to be bound to me. The spear isn't Excalibur. It's my Tesla. But . . . does that mean I have to sleep in the garage from now on?"

There was no way he could sleep in the Tesla's bucket seats, no matter how comfortably they conformed. And sleeping in the garage would be impossible to explain to his parents.

"A better strategy would be to learn to control your dreams, so you don't go spirit walking all the time," said Raven dryly. "Since it doesn't sound like you're much good with a spear."

"So how do I do that?" Jase asked.

"I don't know," she admitted. "The way humans access the interface, that's a human thing. You'll have to deal with it in human ways. But the way you said you were hiding from her search before, I think that means you *can* do it. And you'd better learn quickly. The others may have lost you, but now, in your dreams, Otter Woman can reach you anywhere you go."

The thought sent a chill down Jase's spine—and he was scared enough already.

"Who could teach me how to control my dreams?"

"You know the answer to that," Raven said. "I'll meet you in Valdez, after you've talked to him, and we can heal the sea then."

"Gramps won't even speak to me," Jase protested. "Not unless I admit that my father was totally wrong and he was right. About everything!"

"Was he?" Raven asked curiously. "Right about everything seems like a lot to ask."

"How would I know? It's a complicated issue, and it deals with laws, and stock sales, and all kinds of stuff I don't care about. I do care about my family. And Gramps is part of it," he added grimly. "Whether he admits it or not."

"Tell him that," Raven suggested. "Maybe he'll talk to you then. Because until you learn to control them, your dreams are going to be dangerous. And I mean that in a real, physical sense."

o o o

Jase did sleep in the garage that night, waiting till his parents had gone to bed and then dragging several flat sofa pillows and a blanket down to cushion the concrete floor. When his alarm dragged him out of sleep, at an absurdly early hour, he had a vague memory of crouching in the cave, his shining spear clutched in his hands.

If anything had troubled him there, he had no memory of it.

o o o

He picked Mr. Hillyard up at 6 a.m.—grateful, for once, for the early start. If he made *very* good time after he dropped off his client, Jase could catch the last water shuttle and reach his grandfather's home by 10 p.m. In winter, by that time, it would have been dark for hours and freezing cold, which might have encouraged his grandfather to let him in. In the slanting brilliant sunlight of the summer nights, with a resort full of rooms a twenty-minute hike away that wasn't as likely, but it couldn't hurt to try. In his grandfather's house, under a shaman's protection, maybe he could sleep in a real bed tonight—pillows on concrete left a lot to be desired.

Mr. Hillyard looked more relaxed now that his business was done, though he still had his com board out. They'd been driving for several hours before he shut it down, and looked out the window at the meandering, gravel-bedded river and the white-capped peaks beyond.

"I'll have to come back here sometime for pleasure," he said. "This isn't what I expected."

"What did you expect?" Jase asked. When the client wanted to chat, you chatted.

"I'd heard that the Alcan Highway was nothing but corridors of trees, trees, and more trees."

"Some of the part that runs through Canada is." Jase had driven there too, carrying documents that needed a physical signature, and transportation more discreet than a post office staffed by the signer's brother-in-law.

"But here in Alaska it's almost all open," he went on. "There are stretches where all you see are trees, but the view comes back pretty quickly."

"And then it's spectacular," Mr. Hillyard murmured.

The taiga's appearance hadn't changed, but now that Jase knew how much life seethed through it, it didn't seem ugly anymore. He could hardly tell Mr. Hillyard that.

"So, ah, was this a good trip for you?"

"Oh, yes. Your father's an excellent lawyer. I paid more than I wanted to, but not outrageously. And my integrated community will have a lot less environmental impact than the condos my competitor was planning, so it will be better for the planet too."

"That's good," said Jase, with a sincerity he wouldn't have felt little more than a week ago, when he and Mr. Hillyard had met. "I'm sorry you had to pay more."

"I'm not," said Mr. Hillyard. "Oh, I'd like to have paid a bit less. But the price you're willing to pay is a measure of the value you're buying. And I value what I bought."

Jase frowned. "I thought . . . Doesn't a business always want to pay as little as possible?"

"On one level, yes," the client said. "But unless you're being pretty stupid when you research your investments, you get what you pay for—and one way or another, you pay for what you get! When I was just starting out I picked up an old mall, in what I thought was a fantastic deal. I figured I'd just clean it up a bit and turn it around. Make a huge profit. Turns out it had antiquated energy systems, and some of them were leaking. A quarter-million dollars in rebuilding and environmental impact fees. I was lucky to break even on the project."

"Anyone can be scammed," said Jase sympathetically.

"Probably, but I wasn't scammed. Or if I was, it was me doing the scamming. What I got was worth just about what I'd paid for it. Everything's a tradeoff, one way or the other." Mr. Hillyard leaned back and closed his eyes. "It usually balances out in the end."

So maybe those ancient Ananuts had been on to something. Jase wondered if telling his grandfather that his father was making balanced trades would soften the old man, but he doubted it. And was his grandfather's attitude toward his son so unbalanced because the deal his father had made on behalf of the resort was unbalanced too?

Jase didn't know, but it might be a good question to ask—if he could get his grandfather to open the door in the first place!

o   o   o

Flirting with a speeding ticket all day, Jase reached Valdez in time to catch the last water shuttle with five minutes to spare.

This late shuttle wasn't so crowded, which meant it wouldn't need to make many stops. On the other hand, there was no way to keep the crew from noticing his presence. At least there were no football players onboard.

The girl who was posted at the back of the lounge to answer tourists' questions looked up as Jase came in. Her eyes widened in recognition, and then narrowed in dislike.

He vaguely remembered meeting her at one of the ceremonial feasts his grandfather had insisted he attend. She was pretty, not much older than he was, and she'd been nice, explaining that he didn't have to eat the traditional cakes of pressed fat, that a lot of people surreptitiously dumped them, but that he'd better compliment Mrs. Hennison's fruit of the forest pie. And the pie had been delicious.

Now, making his way to the stable center of the boat, Jase could feel the girl's hostile gaze on his back. Hanging his coat over the seat gave him a chance to look again; she was scowling at him and talking softly into the boat's com mike.

His grandfather was about to learn that Jase was coming. No surprising him.

Jase settled himself with his com pod and waited out the trip. Since it was the last run of the day, when they entered the inlet a steward put the coffee urn on a cart and brought it around, offering passengers a free cup. To reward them for their determination in reaching the resort so late, he said.

It was free, because after this trip they'd have to dump whatever was left in the urn to clean it for tomorrow. Jase, who'd grabbed a fast-food meal to eat in the car almost four hours ago, would have liked a cup. But after a shuttered glance in his direction, the steward pronounced the urn empty just as it reached Jase's row.

He told himself not to be paranoid. It was the end of the day and the urn could simply be empty. But Jase had gotten subtly bad service before, from Natives who recognized his name. It was yet another reason he'd rather spend the night at his grandmother's house than in the resort.

Surely his grandfather, as a shaman, had to help someone who had a problem with spirit-walking dreams?

When Jase got off the shuttle, he saw that the gossip grid had gone into overdrive—his grandmother was waiting on the dock.

"Hello, love." Her hug was warm enough to soothe the sting left by the ferry crew. "I have to say, I wish you hadn't come right now."

"Why? I know it's late, but frankly, I was hoping that might encourage Gramps to put up with me for a night."

"Ordinarily it might, but . . . there's something going on in the village lately. Something I can't put my finger on, but people are angrier at your father, angrier about the resort, than they've been in years. There's even been some vandalism. Traditional symbols of banishment and bad luck painted on the outbuildings, that kind of thing."

Now Jase understood her worried scowl. The resort was the financial mainstay of the village, whether they liked it or not.

"What happened? Did the resort lay down some new policy? Threaten to bus tourists into the village, or cut off the scholarships or something?"

"No. And that's what I can't figure out. There's something stirring people up, but when I talk to them, the ones who're still speaking to me, they can't even say why they're so angry *now*."

"Have you seen any strangers hanging around?" Jase asked.

"No. Just the hotel guests. Why?"

It had been only a few days since he'd healed the taiga. The enemies hadn't found Jase yet, so they couldn't have found his grandparents. "No reason, I just . . . Why are people mad at you? Gramps fought the resort tooth and nail. And you're his wife."

"I'm also your father's mother," she said. "And I refused to take sides between them. I'm on desk duty in the main lodge tonight." For the first time, Jase noticed the crisp uniform blouse under her sweater. "Kathy got sick, and I promised to fill in for her. Or I swear I'd walk you home myself and drag you through that door, no matter what your grandfather says."

"If you're supposed to be at work now, won't you get in trouble?" Adding to his grandmother's problems was the last thing Jase wanted.

"I'm on break," she told him. "If I'm not back on time Lisel will cover for me, but I can't stretch it to forty minutes to walk you home and come back. Probably an hour, if I allow time to argue with your grandfather. I don't get off till midnight, but I'll call and tell him to let you in—and that you'd better be there when I get home! It's my house."

Jase grinned at her. "Then with Gramps being such a traditionalist, I should be there when you get off, shouldn't I? I'll see you later."

She smiled, but the worry lingered in her eyes. "What did you come here for?"

"Those shaman questions I had for Gramps last time have gotten more"—he didn't want to worry her—"interesting. Gima, do you know if anyone in our family, any of my ancestors, had dreams where they walked in the Spirit World?"

He'd become so accustomed to thinking in those terms that he didn't even feel stupid saying it. But her expression closed, as if he'd turned into a stranger.

"Why do you want to know?"

Was this one of those Native cultural things he kept tripping over? But even if this was something you weren't supposed to discuss in public, or with people of a certain age or
gender, surely his grandfather the shaman would talk about it.

"It's part of what I have to ask Gramps," Jase said. "It's for
a . . . a project. Don't worry about it."

The look she cast him then was more worried than it had
been before. "I suppose you have to deal with him. Maybe this
is a good place to start. And Jason? The answer to your question is yes."

She turned and went back to the hotel, presumably to call
her husband and give him admittance orders.

Jase walked down the path past the golf course, feeling
more encouraged than he had for a while. An Ananut matri-
arch, which his grandmother surely was, laid down the rules
for her house.

If he could just talk to the old man, maybe he'd be able to
sleep in a bed tonight! If not, he was heading back to the Tesla,
even if he had to hire a plane to come get him!

At ten in the evening, the sun was running down a slanted
path that would intersect with the northern horizon around
midnight. The trees cast long shadows across the trail, inter-
spersed with patches of golden light, and he heard the soft
rush of waves on the distant beach.

The village seemed to be empty when Jase went through,
which was odd. It was late, on a work night too, but when the
sun was up so long people liked to take advantage of it. Some
people, Ferd was one of them, hardly seemed to need sleep in
the summer.

Jase wasn't one of those people, but he was surprised not to
see more of them out on the streets.

A mop of black fur on long spindly legs lunged at the fence, barking, when Jase went by. A deeper voice bayed in answer somewhere nearby.

The Ananut had never used dogs much. They started their trade circle paddling up the Copper River or down the coast in long dugouts, which they'd obtained trading with their Tlingit neighbors. And although dog sledding was still a popular sport, the days in which every dog in Alaska was a husky were long gone. Jase thought the black mop might be a poodle, without the silly haircut. Another dog, tethered to its shed with a long chain, stared at Jase and then lifted its lip in a silent snarl. It looked to be half Lab, and half something scruffy. All the dogs were properly confined, because dog packs were too dangerous this close to the resort. Aside from the dogs, the village might have been deserted.

Jase actually found himself missing the usual hostile stares.

He marched up the steps to his grandfather's porch, knocked, and was deeply relieved when the door opened.

"Gramps, I'm glad you're here. I need to—"

"Was your father right, to break the corporations and bring in the resort to destroy our way of life?"

"Gima said she was going to call you," Jase protested. "But we can talk about that, and other things too. Inside."

"She did call." His grandfather's mouth tightened. "But it's my house too—tradition be damned! Was your father right?"

"He may have been wrong," said Jase. "About some things. But we're still your fam—"

His grandfather went in and shut the door. Jase threw himself at it, and was twisting the knob when the lock clicked.

"Hey!"

The d-vid came on inside. Jase thought about kicking the

door, but the way his luck was running he'd break his toe, and he refused to spend hours sitting on the steps like an unwanted package. He'd have to go back to the resort and wait for his grandmother to get off her shift.

Jase started back down the street and then stopped. The big black poodle had gotten out, and now stood in the middle of the street, staring at him.

Jase had never had a dog, and he didn't know much about them.

"Good boy," he said. "I'll go around on this side, right?"

With a vague notion of territory, Jase chose the side of the street opposite the dog's yard, but the dog crossed the street to stand in front of him. The low sound it emitted, wavering between a whine and a growl, didn't sound friendly.

Jase looked for its owner, but the street was still empty.

"Hey!" he called. "Your dog's loose."

The d-vid in his grandparents' house was so loud, he could hear it faintly from where he stood, but that was the only human noise.

The poodle trotted toward him, and Jase backed away. The poodle came faster.

Jase ran for the next gate, lifted the simple latch and bolted through, banging it closed behind him just as the poodle arrived.

The dog was growling now, but it was outside the fenced yard—and this fence, designed to discourage deer, was higher than Jase's head.

"Ha," he told the dog. "They'll call your owner to come get you. No treats for you tonight."

Though if fury against his father was running as high as his grandmother said, they might reward the beast as soon as Jase's back was turned. As long as they came and got their dog, he didn't care.

Jase walked up the graveled path to the house. It had mixed flower and vegetable beds beside it, and this early in the year the cabbages were only slightly bigger than normal. Jase would have sworn he saw a curtain at one of the windows twitch as he approached, but no one answered his knock.

A scraping sound made him turn — the poodle was digging at the gravel under the gate.

"You've got to be kidding."

Jase knocked again, louder. These houses had been built almost two centuries ago and most residents, like his grandparents, hadn't even bothered to install doorbells, much less intercoms. But that was because the houses were small enough you could hear it when someone knocked!

Jase banged on the door, no longer caring if it sounded rude, but no one came. The poodle tried to squeeze under the gate, though only its head emerged on the other side.

Jase tried the knob and found the door locked. People in this small safe village hardly ever locked their doors. Maybe the back door would be open. He climbed off the porch and headed around the house.

The poodle was digging more quickly, its curly head matted with dirt from its attempt to crawl under the gate. Without the fancy haircut, it looked more ferocious than any poodle should. Jase increased his pace to a jog and hurried up the steps to the back door — also locked. But the gate at the back of the yard wasn't.

He leaped down the stairs and onto the grass, so his footsteps wouldn't be as audible as they were on gravel. He could sneak away while the poodle was still digging, get a good head start. Surely if its prey was out of sight, the dog wouldn't follow him.

Why had it chased him in the first place? His father hadn't done anything to its way of life. And even if its owners were angry enough to set their dog on three-sixteenths, poodles weren't that kind of dog. Were they?

Taking care not to let the latch clank, Jase eased the gate open. It was in good repair, and didn't creak when he closed it behind him.

The houses were close enough that Jase could hurry down the alley behind the cottages without the dog at the front gate catching sight of him. Jase hoped the stupid thing dug for hours, and that the house's owner tripped in the hole—serve them both right!

Most of the houses looked more ragged from the back, but that may have been because that side faced the beach, and salt spray took a toll even on modern paint.

Jase was halfway down the street, when he saw the Lab mix who'd snarled trotting toward him.

One dog escaping to chase him was coincidence. Two dogs escaping . . . Jase took to his heels and ran. He'd cut back to his grandparents' house, and break the front window if he had to!

But when he reached an unfenced passage between the alley and the street, the poodle was there. It began to bark, but Jase no longer needed subtle clues. He ran down the alley, heading for the path that followed the base of the rocky bluffs that lined the beach opposite the sea. He'd scrambled up those bluffs as a child, while Gima dug up edible stuff in the tidal flats, and there were places no dog could climb after him.

He'd forgotten how far those places were. Jase looked back. Four dogs loped behind him now, the poodle, the Lab mix, something that looked mostly husky, and a ridiculous beagle scurrying behind the others.

It should have looked comical, but something about the way they paced themselves, keeping the beagle with them, told Jase this was a *pack*.

Dog packs were some of the most deadly predators on the planet, no matter how motley their breeds.

Jase was still several hundred yards from the nearest bluff when the dogs flattened out and began to run—he'd thought they were moving fast before, but they'd just been jogging!

He would never reach the bluff in time. Looking around frantically, Jase spotted a dead pine at the edge of the forest. It had probably been killed by lightning, but enough low branches remained for him to climb it.

Jase raced for the tree, faster than he'd ever run in his life. Those branches were higher than they'd looked from a distance, but he jumped and caught the lowest. His slick-soled chauffeur shoes scrabbled for purchase on the smooth trunk and caught just enough for him to haul himself into the tree as the dogs dashed up below him.

The husky took a running leap and grabbed one shoe, pulling it from his foot, and Jase found himself three branches higher before he even thought about moving.

The dogs stared up at him with conscienceless eyes. The husky dropped his shoe and sat, clearly prepared to wait. The beagle was panting hard, but its gaze was no less determined than the others'.

No matter what they wanted, they couldn't reach him. Clinging to the trunk with both arms, Jase finally had time to think.

His heart was trying to pound its way out of his rib cage,

and his legs still shook with the effort of the chase. His hands were shaking too, from terror and adrenaline, as he pulled out his com pod and thumbed it on. The screen remained dark.

That battery was supposed to be good for five years!

Jase tried to breathe more slowly, and then tried the pod again. No power. No low battery alerts over the last few weeks to warn him to replace it, either. Could the battery have shifted out of contact during the chase?

Mindful of the attentive dogs below, Jase took off his blazer, carefully maintaining his hold on the tree, which made it tricky. But the battery was small; he didn't dare risk dropping it.

Jase opened the pod's case and pulled the circuitry card that held the battery—still snapped neatly into its socket. He turned the plastic wafer over his jacket and flexed it gently till the battery popped out. Examining the slim silver disk, Jase couldn't see any leakage or corrosion. He snapped it back into the card and checked the wafer itself. Nothing appeared to be broken. The other wafer held the small screen, and Jase looked it over too, but saw nothing broken there either. All the receptor points looked clean. So why wasn't it working?

He snapped the pod back together and tried to turn it on, but the screen remained blank. "Carp."

He looked down at the dogs. Three of them were sitting by the base of the tree—only the poodle prowled restlessly.

The tree Jase had chosen was on a rise, and the lowering sun cast the dogs' shadows onto the beach below, tall and distorted. Something about the poodle's shadow caught Jase's eye. The long thin legs seemed to stretch forever, but its body looked bulkier than it should . . . and instead of flopping down, like the dog's ears did, the shadow had pointed triangular ears.

Jase rubbed his eyes and looked again, but even though the poodle's ears fell past its narrow jaw, the shadow's ears were small, upright, and pricked. One of the shadow ears twitched as he watched, and both the poodle and its shadow turned, seeking the source of some sound he hadn't heard.

Now that he was looking, the Lab's shadow had angular pricked ears as well—even the beagle, with its short coat and stubby legs, cast the shadow of a wolf.

The hair on Jase's arms stood up as goose flesh popped out on most of his body.

The enemy had found him.

He didn't have time to wait for his grandmother to come home, realize that Jase hadn't gone back to take a room at the resort, and then organize anyone who hadn't been bewitched. Now he knew what, *who,* had been stirring up the villagers!

But whatever search party his grandmother raised, it wouldn't get here before his enemies did. And he'd be here when Otter Woman and the football players arrived. The dogs, with their wolf shadows, would see to that.

Despite the urgency of the moment, wonder washed over Jase. This wasn't invisible healing on some invisible ley. This was real magic, in the real, daylight world.

Magic that might kill him, if he couldn't escape.

Why hadn't he figured out some way to contact Raven! But even if he had her com code, it wouldn't help him now. When her enemies showed up, Jase should hand over the pouch just to serve her right for being so shortsighted!

He didn't want to hand it over.

That old woman, Otter Woman, had upset his grandmother laying this trap. And she'd made Jase's grandfather, the whole village, more angry with his father—just on the chance that he'd come here and she could capture him. But how could he—

A scratching sound drew his eyes to the foot of the tree. The poodle was digging again, this time at the base of the trunk, and a chill ran over Jase's skin as he saw how this looser dirt flew from under its busy paws.

The husky, whose shadow almost matched its form, got up and started digging too, and then the Lab and the beagle joined in.

How much was left of the roots that held this tree upright? It felt sturdy, but the lack of bark told him it had died a long time ago.

They can't kill you themselves, Raven had said. *But they're a lot more adept at using human tools than I thought they'd be.*

Maybe the plan wasn't to use the dogs to keep him pinned till they could come for him. Maybe it was to take the pouch off his mangled corpse after the dogs—tools of this world—had done the job for them. If Jase understood the setup correctly, their fracking rules would allow that just fine.

He had to get out of here. But how? He had a pouch of magical healing dust hanging around his neck. Could it break spells, as well as heal leys?

Jase pulled out his com pod and tried to connect with it, with its essence, as he had in the taiga. He wasn't attached to his pod like he was to the Tesla, but machines did feel . . . there to him. He reached out to that feeling of presence, and took a tight grip on the tree trunk. If the power surge he'd felt in the taiga knocked him off his branch, he was done for. Fumbling, because he had to use the arm that was wrapped around the trunk to hold the pod, he pulled out the pouch and extracted a pinch of dust.

"Work," he whispered, and scattered the dust over the com pod.

No power slammed through him this time, but hope still flickered as he pressed the on button. Nothing.

Frack.

He tried the dogs next, climbing down to the lowest branch and dumping a small handful of dust on the beagle's back—he wasn't about to descend and try to bond with them!

The beagle, busily deepening the hole at the base of the tree, didn't even look up. Its wolf shadow never wavered.

The poodle had stopped digging to watch him descend. Now it leaped up, higher than the husky had, and Jase kicked it away.

It yelped and fell, but Jase was now watching the shadows as warily as he watched the dogs, and as the poodle landed its shadow changed to that of a curly-haired dog with floppy ears.

It shook itself, whining in confusion, and that other shadow flowed over the true one. But sudden pain had shocked it out of the spell, at least for a moment. And they could be hurt.

Was it his imagination that the tree felt less sturdy now than when he'd climbed it? Jase hated the idea of hurting some helpless enchanted dog—but not as much as he hated the idea of the four of them ripping him apart.

He climbed carefully back up the tree and broke off the biggest branch he could manage. It might be just that he was moving pretty wildly, in a higher part of the tree, but it wobbled in a way that told him he didn't have much time.

Jase buttoned his blazer, for whatever protection it might provide, and descended to the lowest branch.

"OK, dog. Want to jump again?"

Poodles were supposed to be smart, and this one lived up to

the rep. It looked up at him for a moment and then went back to digging.

The tree was definitely wobbling now. Jase gripped the branch with both legs and one hand, leaned down as far as he dared, and swung his improvised club.

It struck the Lab's shoulder, knocking it into a yelping roll. But it lunged to its feet, snarling, and leaped at Jase where he dangled from the tree.

This time Jase was ready, and swung the branch as hard as he could. In sheer self-preservation he aimed for the dog's head, but wielding the heavy branch one-handed, he hit its nose instead.

It fell to the ground with a sharp cry of pain . . . and the pricked ears vanished from its shadow.

The Lab licked its nose, whimpering, then dropped into a crouch and scuttled away.

He could break the spell! And if he didn't, they'd kill him. Jase leaned down, aiming for the poodle next, but he'd underestimated the pack.

The husky jumped up and locked its teeth on Jase's sleeve, its whole weight dangling from his right arm. Jase gripped the branch with all the strength of his desire to survive . . . and the tree began to tip.

Slowly at first, slowly enough for Jase to swing the growling husky against the tree's trunk hard enough to make the dog let go. Slowly enough for Jase to release the branch with his legs, swing down to land on his feet, and scramble out of the dogs' hole.

He smacked the beagle hard on its muddy snout as he darted past, and it yipped, but Jase was too busy racing out of the path of the falling giant to check its shadow.

He ran to the nearest tree, a live one, and put his back against the trunk before the echoes of the crash had faded. Only the husky and the poodle stalked him now. The husky circling aggressively, waiting for a chance to spring, the poodle prancing out of reach of the stick, watching him with bright, intent eyes.

Jase went for the husky since it was closest. This time he was aiming for the dog's nose, so of course he missed and struck its head. The dog sank to the ground, its eyes half closed. Hopefully he'd only stunned it—but better for it to die than him!

Jase stepped away from the tree and went after the poodle, quickly, hoping to take it out before the others' wolf shadows returned.

"Come on. You want me?" He was shouting now, not sure if he hoped to drive it off or force it to attack. The poodle backed up, but its predatory gaze never shifted.

A roar shattered the stillness, and the poodle flinched.

Jase stumbled back to the tree, club raised, as a grizzly erupted from the forest and roared again.

The dogs fled, the husky stumbling behind the other three. Jase didn't have any attention to spare for their shadows now. He'd have run with them, but running wouldn't save him.

If the grizzly was determined to kill him, nothing Jase could do would stop it, but the experts said it was better to fight than to do nothing.

Jase gripped his club and waited. Maybe it would ignore him. Maybe it would go away. He was trying not to breathe when a rush of wings hurtled down through the branches.

The raven lit on the tip of his club, heavier than he'd expected. Then it dropped to the ground, bulged, and grew into a slender naked girl.

Who stood between him and the bear.

"Get behind me," Jase hissed, even as he prayed she had some magic to deal with this.

She glanced back over her shoulder and flashed him a smile, then turned to the great beast, who'd settled on its haunches.

"You see what I mean?" she said. "If this isn't 'direct interference,' I don't know what is."

"We tol' them they can't attack your human themselvez. For this, they're uzing the toolz of this world. Azzz allowed." The bear's mouth didn't handle English very well, and goose flesh broke out on Jase's arms once more—though a shapeshifter, even one speaking English in animal form, was a lot less scary than a grizzly bear. Jase kept the branch, just in case.

"They may be using the tools of this world," Raven said, "but they've also used a lot of ley power, both in setting up this trap and springing it. If they can draw power from the ley then I'll have to do it too. And I don't want to weaken the leys more than they already are."

"True." The bear looked thoughtful. "Unnaseptable. We'll deal with them. They'll spen' no more power in this world. Not an erg more."

"You speak for the neutrals?" Raven asked hopefully.

"It will be our edic'."

The bear nodded its massive head, rose, and lumbered back into the woods. Jase lowered the branch. His fingers were so stiff, it felt like he had to peel them away from the rough surface.

Raven turned, her face alight with joy.

"You did it!"

CHAPTER 8

"Why can't you ever be naked when I'm in shape to appreciate it," Jase grumbled. He'd given her his blazer so her nudity would stop distracting him — it didn't seem to bother her. She walked down the trail beside him as if the rocks didn't hurt her bare feet at all. It had taken Jase five minutes to locate the shoe the husky had stolen, in the wreckage of the tree.

Soon they'd be walking on the sandy beach, bypassing the village. Jase didn't want to meet any more dogs.

"Do you realize what this means?" Raven was bubbling with excitement. "Bear, who has great influence among the neutrals, is going to enforce the edict that none of the others can use ley energy in this world! He's already forbidden them to threaten you themselves. Without ley power, they can't manipulate anything that belongs to this dimension. No more mind-slaved bikers! No more attack dogs! We'll be able to finish healing this ley with no trouble at all, assuming you can reach it through sea and air. You didn't drop the pouch or anything, right?"

"Of course not." Jase felt to make sure it was still there as he spoke. "I used some of the dust trying to break the spell on those dogs, but — "

"How much did you use?"

"Not too much." Jase pulled out the pouch to show her. "I couldn't touch them, so I thought it would take—"

"It's half gone! How could you waste it like that?"

"I was trying to save my life," said Jase, nettled. "I didn't have any way to get in touch with you, so I had to improvise. There's plenty left for two more healings. It only took a pinch in the taiga. And it's not like . . . Ah, you don't need this for other leys, do you?"

"No," said Raven. "That dust is matched to the signature of this ley, and healing this ley is all it does. So don't go tossing it over your car!"

"I wouldn't have had to use it on the dogs, if I'd had some way to reach you," Jase pointed out. "How do I get in touch with you when I need to?"

She could hardly deny it was necessary, after today.

"That's tricky," Raven admitted. "Even if you bought me one of those pod-stick things, I'd have to abandon it the next time I changed form or went home. And I've got to go home soon," she added. "I want to make sure Bear doesn't leave any loopholes for them to squeeze through, and that everyone who opposes me gets the message. Once I've done that, we can heal the next two nexuses this weekend. And no one will be able to stop us."

They'd reached the beach while she was speaking, and waves rushed and receded beside them. Jase thought he could find the sea's life energy without much trouble. Air . . . Well, he'd have time to try again, if he needed to.

"What about my dreams?" he asked. "According to you, I'm not in this world then."

"True," said Raven. "But I'm sure I can convince the neutrals that killing you is direct interference no matter where they do it. If they kill my chosen healer, then according to our agreement they give up any right to meddle in this world and I'm free to do whatever I like. If I go now, you'll be able to sleep sound tonight."

"So if you can't use a com pod, how do I get in touch with you?" Jase persisted. "There's got to be some shapeshifter way."

"There are several," Raven admitted. "But I'd have to use ley energy to create any of them, and right now I don't dare use even a spark! Not if I'm going to win my argument. If you need to talk to me, tie a bright-colored rag to the balcony rail near your window and I'll contact you as soon as I can."

That would be easier to explain than a sign saying "Call me," but . . .

"It's awfully low-tech," Jase complained. "Low-magic, too."

Her clear laugh pealed out. "You don't have enough magic in your life right now? Besides, you can handle most things yourself. You just proved that, in case you hadn't noticed."

Jase brightened. "I did take out all but the poodle, didn't I?"

"You'd have taken down that ferocious poodle too, in a few more minutes." She managed to keep her voice sober, but the warm dark eyes danced.

"Hey, that poodle was ferocious! And their shadows . . . What happened to those dogs?"

"Those shadows were the visible manifestation of the aspect of the wolf." She'd turned serious now. "And inducing that aspect, which all dogs carry, was a necessary part of their trap. Because those dogs, in their true being, would never even bite a human, much less kill one."

Cold crept over Jase once more. "And in wolf mode they would have?"

"Yes," said Raven. "But you stopped them. And when Bear saw what they'd done, it tipped the balance in our favor. Without the neutral's intervention—"

"Jase!" The shout came from far down the beach. He looked up and saw his grandmother emerge from the woods and start toward him.

"Go back to Anchorage," Raven told him. "I'll contact you as soon as it's safe to start the next healing."

She'd stepped behind him, which was fine for now, but how was he going to explain this near-naked girl to his grandmother?

"If we're safe now, make it next weekend." Jase waved to the older woman. "I don't think I'll be in the mood to commune with nature for a while. But how are we going to get out of this?"

There was no answer. When he turned to look back, his blazer lay crumpled on the sand.

o   o   o

She could have shifted into a sand flea, or even just disintegrated and gone back to her own dimension. If you could "manifest your physicality" whenever you chose, presumably you could unmanifest as well.

Jase folded the jacket over his arm so his grandmother wouldn't see the rents left by the husky's teeth, and told her that his grandfather had refused to talk to him, and he'd decided to take a room at the resort after all. He'd go back to Anchorage in the morning.

She protested, but even in the silvery twilight Jase could see the weariness of a shift that had ended at midnight, and the deeper, more painful exhaustion of dealing with the gulf between her husband and her son.

Had he added to that grief? Or was she glad that he was still trying?

It felt awkward, but Jase kissed her cheek in parting. The next time his mother came down to visit Gima, he'd go with her. He might not be able to solve the problem, but he could help them try.

o   o   o

Jase fell into a bed at the resort, slept through the night, and reached Anchorage just in time for dinner. He made sure that his father's firm had no driving jobs for him that weekend, and felt his face heat at the knowing look his parents exchanged. But he was going on a date with Raven, sort of. Maybe he could bring a picnic too, and a couple of soft, thick blankets!

o   o   o

Halfway through Friday-morning algebra, one of the school's councilors pulled Jase out of class and told him that his grandmother was being flown to Anchorage General, and his parents wanted him to meet them there.

Jase broke speed limits all the way to the hospital, but he didn't care. What could have happened to Gima? The councilor hadn't known any details beyond the message she'd delivered. His grandmother had looked tired and stressed, but she hadn't seemed to be ill. Not in pain or out of breath. Even if some remnant of the enemies' spell had lingered in the village, Jase couldn't believe anyone would harm his grandmother. There was always the possibility of an accident, but the resort's medics could treat most injuries. In fact, they could handle everything short of major surgery, and part of the deal his father had made for the resort included medical treatment for all local residents.

So whatever it was, it must be serious.

Jase slammed the Tesla to a stop in the first parking space he found and hurried into the hospital. He was in sight of the information desk when his mother intercepted him. Her mouth was tight with worry, but she wasn't weeping, and Jase's worst fear eased.

"What happened to Gima? Will she be all right?"

"Your grandmother's in a coma." His mother's voice was determinedly level. "She didn't wake up this morning, and when your grandfather couldn't wake her he called the medics. They haven't found a cause yet, but her breathing, heart, all her vital signs are stable, and they're running brain scans now. We should get the results any time."

She led him into the elevator as she spoke, pressing the button for the sixteenth floor.

"How did this happen?" Jase asked. "She was fine a few days ago."

"That's one of the things they don't know yet," his mother said. "I just hope your father and grandfather don't say something unforgivable before she wakes up."

Jase stared at her. "Surely they're too worried about Gima to fight with each other now."

"You'd think so," said his mother wearily. "But when he first discovered he couldn't rouse her, your grandfather tried some Native awakening ceremonies to . . . call her back, was how he put it. For some types of coma getting her into medical care quickly doesn't matter much. But for some kinds," she finished grimly, "it can make the difference between life and death."

"Carp," Jase whispered. "Does Dad know about that?"

"I got him out of the room just before he accused Gramps to his face of killing his own wife through 'superstitious ignorance.' And I shut him up, for the time being, by pointing out that waiting a few hours to call the medics might not have made any difference. We'd better hope that's true," she finished. "For all kinds of reasons."

There were tears in her eyes now, and a lump rose in Jase's throat. If Gima died . . .

He put his arm around his mother, not sure if he was trying to support her or clinging for comfort. It hardly mattered.

They stepped out of the elevator together, and Jase saw his father and grandfather standing on either side of a man with a white coat over his suit.

" . . . so in a sense," the doctor was saying, "this is encouraging news. The fact that there's nothing wrong with her brain, no stroke, no tumors, no neural damage, that means that when she regains consciousness there's an excellent chance she'll be all right. We just need to find out why she's not waking up."

"I keep telling you!" His grandfather's voice was hoarse with worry and frustration. "She's spirit walking!"

The fine hairs on the back of Jase's neck prickled at the words, and his grandfather went on, "I admit, I don't understand why she's not coming back. But unless you've got a medicine that can smooth a spirit's path back to the body, you need to let me do some calling rituals!"

Jase's father drew in a breath to speak, but his wife wrapped both arms around him, murmuring urgently, and he subsided. His face was gray with fatigue and fear, and Jase almost went to hug him too. But his grandfather looked even worse, unshaven, in rumpled clothes. The lines on his face had deepened as if he'd aged ten years overnight.

And Jase had a terrible sinking feeling that in this case his father might be wrong.

The doctor considered the matter more thoughtfully than Jase had expected. "I can't see that it would do any harm. If your calling ritual involves any stimulants, even if they're in smoke form or absorbed through the skin, I'll have to screen and OK them. The last thing we want is some herbal med reacting with whatever we decide to try. But if it's just chanting and drums, that certainly wouldn't hurt her."

"I need to paint the return path onto her body," his grandfather said. "The paints are natural, no drugs in them. Nothing to be cleared."

"If you're painting on her skin I want to analyze them first," the doctor said firmly. "There might be physiological effects you don't know about."

"There's an entire world of knowledge he doesn't know about," Jase's father said bitterly. "And I'm not about to stand by while he delays my mother's real treatment with his idiocy! Doctor, what should we do next?"

"Well," said the doctor, "before I recommend any treatment we need to find the—"

"I already know why she's not waking up!" His grandfather's pallor had vanished, but Jase wasn't sure the angry flush that replaced it was an improvement. "I can sense the cord of light that binds her spirit to her body and will guide her back. I just don't know why it's taking so long this time."

This time? Had his grandmother gone spirit walking before? She'd said one of his ancestors was a spirit walker! Why hadn't she told him she was talking about herself?

"But as long as her spirit journeys, nothing you do will make any difference," his grandfather continued. "You're the ignorant ones!"

He'd used the plural, but he was looking at Jase's father.

"Gramps. Michael." His mother stepped between them. "It sounds like we've got some time. Why don't you and I get a cup of coffee, Gramps, and you can tell me about these rituals. Jase, take your father for a walk."

Jase laid a hand on his father's arm and found the muscles rigid with fury. Lawyerlike, he was masking most of what he felt, but he was about to erupt. And when Gima woke up, the quarrel she'd spent most of Jase's life trying to mend might have become unmendable.

"Come on, Dad, let's get out of here. Fresh air."

For a moment he was afraid it wouldn't work, but his mother had her own form of power. His father turned and walked away, so abruptly Jase had to scramble after him.

There was a park beside the hospital, where Jase spent the better part of the next hour watching his father pace and rant about "Stone Age superstitions" and "traditions that strangle whole towns."

This wasn't the moment to tell his father that Jase had been doing some spirit walking himself, lately. In fact, that day might never come.

They talk about how hard it is for a Native, growing up in a white man's world, his father had said to him once. *Believe me, growing up a lawyer in a Native world is no easier.*

His father had fought his way out of that world, working

furiously to get into law school, and after he graduated, too. And he'd tried to make it easier for other Native kids to follow his path.

Jase couldn't say he was wrong about that, no matter what his grandfather demanded.

However, this time his grandfather was right. Almost right. Jase's grandmother's spirit wasn't just out walking. She'd been kidnapped.

CHAPTER 9

IT WAS NIGHT BEFORE JASE managed to escape from the hospital. His father and grandfather had resolved their immediate dilemma by communicating through Jase's mother. Since the doctor's next set of tests was scheduled for tomorrow, his grandfather had gone home to collect his ritual paraphernalia for the lab to screen. Jase's father had chosen to stay in Gima's room, holding her hand and talking to her. *A white man's calling ritual,* his mother had said. She was trying to placate both sides, and ended up irritating both of them—though Jase thought she was right.

He'd almost asked to go with his grandfather. They needed to discuss this! But after Jase had sided with his father for so many years, would his grandfather even believe him?

The old man was going to try to get her back, using every shaman technique he knew, anyway. But Jase didn't think it would work. The Spirit World was Otter Woman's territory, more than any human's. It would take more than a calling ritual to beat her.

His mother rode home with him to pack some overnight gear, and then she returned to the hospital to stay with her husband. Leaving Jase, finally, alone in the house.

He was exhausted to his bones, but he'd never be able to sleep. His mother didn't approve of them, but his father kept some mild sleeping pills that he sometimes used the night before critical, complex negotiations.

Jase downed two of them, opened his closet door, and fell into bed.

It didn't take long.

The old woman, Otter Woman, stepped out of the closet smiling. Jase suddenly realized he'd never really hated anyone before. He'd thought he had, but this deep, cold desire to annihilate was something he'd never experienced.

"I thought direct interference was against the rules," he said.

"Interference with you, yes. Using the power of the leys in your world, yes. But I've done nothing to you, and this"—she gestured to his bedroom, where leafy twigs were beginning to sprout from the furniture—"I don't need to use any ley power here."

"Do you have any idea how much you're hurting my family?" His voice shook with sheer rage.

"You know, I didn't expect you to figure it out this quickly. You're fairly bright, for a human."

"It wasn't hard," said Jase. "Most thugs aren't as smart as they think they are. What do you want?"

"You know what I want, boy. Give me the pouch. Give me that accursed effective catalyst, and we'll let your grandmother go."

"Go back to her body?" Jase could think of several different places a detached spirit might go, and he didn't want

his grandmother's spirit being given a push in the wrong direction.

"Go wherever she chooses," said Otter Woman. "She's trying to get back to her body now. Her failure appears to be . . . painful."

Horror swamped Jase's anger. "You're hurting her! You think you're so superior to humans, but no human would—"

Her laughter was rich and cruel. "No, you can't say a human would never do that. And we're just holding her here. It's her own struggle that causes the pain. If she'd stop fighting, she'd stop hurting."

Gima would never stop fighting.

"So if I give you the dust, you'll let her go? Your word, enforced by Bear and the neutrals, that you'll let her go if I hand over that pouch."

"Of course," said Otter Woman. "You have my word. The catalyst is all we want."

"Done," said Jase. "When and where do we meet?"

When Jase woke the next morning, the first thing he did was dive into his closet and drag out the Hawaiian shirt he'd picked up two vacations ago and never worn since. A few snips of the scissors and ripping tugs reduced it to long rags.

Jase padded out to the deck, ignoring the cold wood under his bare feet, and tied three bright strips to the balcony rail.

If that didn't make the *contact me immediately* message clear, well, he'd given her a chance.

He called the hospital, in case he was wrong, but there was "no change" in Mrs. Mintok's condition. He called his mother, hoping she had more information. The only thing that had changed since he'd left was that his grandfather—who'd driven a rental car all night—had returned, and the techs were analyzing his paints right now.

She'd had to drag his father out of the building, and could Jase bring . . .

Jase wrote down the items, paying so little attention she had to repeat herself twice.

If his grandfather succeeded, he wouldn't have to do this! But unless he succeeded quickly, Jase didn't dare risk waiting too long.

If he made this trade with Otter Woman, and his grandmother returned in the middle of his grandfather's ritual, would that make his father more tolerant? No, he'd call it sheer coincidence. And Jase's grandfather would be even less inclined to admit that the old ways weren't always best.

Carp. He'd worry about that when his grandmother was back.

Jase was downing a quick-heat sandwich and pulling clothing out of his father's dresser when he heard the knock, not from the front door, but on the glass door that opened to the deck.

Raven wore the familiar stretchie and jeans—did she store them somewhere near his house? Today she hadn't bothered with the flannel shirt, and her feet were bare.

"I know what happened to your grandmother." She started talking before the door was fully open. "Why didn't you tell me you weren't the only spirit walker in your family?"

"I didn't know. And don't tell me I should have paid more attention to my heritage. Is she all right? Is she . . . is she hurting?"

Are they hurting her?

"She's all right," said Raven. "And as far as hurting . . . She's frightened, she's frustrated, and she's a prisoner. She seemed pretty calm, all things considered. I wasn't allowed to talk to her. I barely managed to see her! But she's fine for now. How long can a human's spirit survive, separated from its body? And how long can your bodies survive when they're empty?"

"I don't know. With the body . . . they can keep people's bodies running for a long time."

The thought of his grandmother lying still and silent for years, with tubes pumping life into her, made Jase flinch.

"But Gima doesn't need that. She's breathing on her own. I think she's even swallowing. Her body should be OK, as long as we get her back quickly."

He was looking right at her as he spoke, so he didn't miss the moment Raven's eyes flicked aside.

"Damn it, you have to get her back! What about all those rules against interfering with me? What about Bear and the neutrals? What about your allies, Frog guy and Goose Woman?"

"Frog People and Goose Woman can't help with this. The problem is, what they've done isn't against the rules," said Raven. "Not quite. They haven't simply killed you, or taken the pouch. They aren't using ley power from this world—in fact, they're not using any ley's power. They are using a tool of this world, but that's still within our original agreement. If I can use a human as my healer, they can use humans too. Though I'll argue that this wasn't the kind of use anyone had in mind when the agreement was made."

"So how long will it take you to get her free? One day? Two?"

"There was a reason I asked how long her body and spirit

could survive apart," Raven admitted. "This is a delicate negotiation. It's going to take time."

Jase's dad worked on delicate negotiations, so he knew more about them than he wanted to.

"What if we went out and healed the ley right now? They'd have no reason to hold her. Would they let her go? Or would they kill her?"

Raven shook her head slowly. "Humans don't usually mean much to them either way. But you've managed to annoy them sufficiently that I think they're looking for revenge. Yes, if we just go out and heal the ley, they'll kill her."

Another thing Jase knew from watching his father deal with delicate negotiations was that the reason they were so delicate was because you might lose.

"Thanks for telling me the truth," he said. "I know it would be easier to lie."

Raven grimaced. "I thought about it. But if we healed the sea, and then you got a call from your mother saying your grandmother had just died, would you go on and heal the air?"

"I'd flush that dust down the nearest toilet," Jase said. "I'd burn it. I'd do everything I could to make sure no one could use it, ever again."

"That's what I figured," Raven said. "In fact, in your shoes, that's what I'd do. That's why I'll go back home, and talk and keep on talking till I convince the neutrals that with humans this *is* direct interference!"

"Are you sure you can convince them?"

"Yes." Her eyes met his in that too-direct, too-steady look that practiced liars used. "I'll get her freed. I promise. Because I know you won't go on with the healing if I don't."

She would try. He knew she'd try. But she shouldn't have

met his gaze just then, for in the depths of her dark eyes he saw despair.

And she wasn't the only one who could lie.

"All right," said Jase. "I'll make sure they don't do anything rash at the hospital. But get her back as quick as you can. I think my father and grandfather are about to start swinging."

o   o   o

He drove to the hospital and delivered his father's clothes. His mother had persuaded her husband to go to the office, and take care of everything that needed to be dealt with so he could spend some time away.

In his father's absence, she and Jase helped Gramps with his rituals, bringing him a few things he still needed, like water fresh from a living stream. When there was nothing else they could do, they kept the nurses out of the room.

His grandfather held on to a shaman's calm, but Jase could see his fear, his grief, growing as the first ritual failed, and then the next.

After several hours had passed, Jase slipped away and left them to it.

His grandfather was doing everything he could, and it wasn't working. Jase had one more thing to do before going to meet with Otter Woman.

o   o   o

They'd agreed on Potter Marsh as a place both of them could locate. It was also, Jase thought, a place he might be able to see the football players coming—though he didn't need to. He was going to give them what they wanted.

This should be easy.

Clouds and sun fought for control of the sky, with a brisk wind assisting. It ruffled the water's surface and forced the swallows into wild acrobatics. It also cut down on the tourists. Only a handful of people were out on the boardwalks today, huddled into their jackets and wishing they'd worn something warmer.

Jase went to the end of the longest boardwalk and stood, ignoring the fact that his ears were freezing. She didn't keep him waiting long.

The old woman wore modern pants and boots, and a rain jacket that was too big for her, though it probably cut the wind. He'd thought she might bring the football players as bodyguards, though he was pretty sure Otter Woman was the boss. And she didn't need bodyguards. Seeing his dream come to life, walking casually over the wooden planks in the daylight world, was almost as frightening as being chased by the Olmaat. At least the monster had the decency to stay in the nightmare world, where it belonged.

The world in which his grandmother was trapped. Was she being stalked by the Olmaat now? At least no injuries had appeared on the body that lay in that hospital bed. Because she hadn't "manifested" any of her physical being in the Spirit World? Or because they hadn't started tormenting her yet?

Jase had to make sure they never did.

"You'll let her go?" he demanded as Otter Woman approached. "She'll wake up, and be all right?"

"If you give me the catalyst I have no reason to keep her," the old woman said. "Do you have it?"

"That's not a promise."

"I already promised. If you like, I'll do it again. Do you have the medicine bag?"

Jase had no way to enforce a promise, even if she repeated it. He pulled the pouch out of his pocket, the soft leather still warm from the heat of his body. Holding it out to her wasn't easy—it felt worse than anything he'd ever done in his life.

Otter Woman took the pouch, frowned, and clenched her hand around it.

"There's hardly any left. What happened to the rest? If you've kept some of it back, human, I'll know it. And—"

"I didn't," said Jase. He'd thought about that, but he'd been afraid she'd know, this woman who dominated his dreams. She would punish his grandmother if he tried. "I poured most of it over the batteries in my car. Raven rigged it so the Tesla won't run unless the dust is there and I'm there. I can't afford to lose my transport now."

If Raven was telling the truth, his car would die in a few weeks anyway, when the dust wasn't "properly used." At that point Jase could replace the enchanted batteries with new ones, that didn't go around imagining they were cold all the time. It would be expensive, but running a vintage Tesla was expensive.

He was already paying a higher price than that.

Otter Woman threw back her head and laughed. "How like Raven, to try to fix the game that way. And if you really scattered it—yes, I see you did—you could never gather up enough of the pollens to use it. How very fitting, that breaking her own meddling destroyed it!"

Smiling still, she wrapped the cords around the pouch, pulled back her arm, and hurled it toward the sky.

Despite himself Jase lurched after it—but it didn't fall.

In a great rush of feathers, an eagle swooped down and snatched the pouch out of the air. Some of the distant tourists shouted, but Jase ignored them. The big brown bird flapped away till it was only a brown dot in his vision. Then the dot vanished.

His head ached. His heart ached. He turned grimly back to Otter Woman, but she'd already turned away, walking back down the boardwalk to the parking lot. And truly, there was nothing left to say.

The deal was done.

CHAPTER 10

JASE HAD JUST PARKED THE Tesla in the hospital's garage when he heard the thump of running steps and looked up to see Raven hurrying toward him. She wore rumpled surgical scrubs, probably pulled from some hospital laundry bin. And either there were feathers woven into her sleek hair, or some parts of her hadn't yet shifted into human form.

"What happened? I felt the pouch leave you, and now I can't sense it at all! Did you—"

"I gave it to Otter Woman." Jase's voice was hoarse, and he cleared his throat before he went on. "In exchange for my grandmother. So you're going to have to—"

Her warm dark skin turned muddy tan when she paled. "You *what?* I told you I'd get her back!"

"You said you'd try," said Jase. "But don't pretend you believed you were going to succeed. Even I could see you didn't think you'd get her back."

"So what!" Her voice echoed in the concrete cavern. "She's only one human woman, who'll die in a handful of decades anyway. I'm trying to save a whole living world!"

"And I'm trying to save one old woman," said Jase flatly. "Because to me, she matters more. You'll find some other way to heal the leys."

"I told you, that dust can't be replaced! It has to be human magic that—"

"Carpo!" Jase snapped. "You could do it yourself, with your own damn magic, if you weren't so busy playing politics with your sadistic kidnapping friends. It's a game, to all of you. But it's not a game to my grandfather and my family. And to me, they matter more."

Mr. Hillyard was right. You paid for what you wanted. The more important it was, the higher the price.

"Playing politics," Raven said, in a voice he'd never heard from her before. "Maybe we are, but that doesn't make the game less real or the stakes less deadly. You're a traitor, Jason Mintok. Like your father. And it's not just me you've betrayed."

She turned and stalked away. Her bare feet were dirty from the grimy floor.

"Where are you going?" Jase was angry enough, hurt enough, that he wanted to go on shouting at her, even if it wouldn't do any good.

"Home," she yelled back. "Home to find out where in this world they've hidden that pouch. And then I'm going to find a better human to carry it!"

"Fine! I hope you do. I hope he's fracking Galahad. I just hope you don't get half of his family killed too!"

She kept walking, and in only moments turned out of sight. In another minute she'd melt and disappear.

Jase would have kicked the Tesla, but he didn't want to risk scraping the finish.

She'd find the pouch eventually. In this world, she'd said, which made sense. If he couldn't take a weapon into the Spirit World, if she couldn't take clothing to and from it, then the pouch would have to stay here too. She would find it, and then find some other poor sucker to heal the sea, and the air, and whatever else she wanted healed.

Jase was done with it.

He'd never claimed he was a hero. He'd tried to tell her that, at first. Not his fault she'd refused to listen.

Jase went up to his grandmother's room and watched her sleep. She might wake up any minute now, though he couldn't explain that to his parents, who wandered in and out badgering the doctors about more tests.

He might have explained it to his grandfather, but the old man was so focused on his wife that Jase didn't think he could get his attention. There would be time to talk, to tell his story and ask questions later, when his grandmother was awake and safe in her own home.

But she didn't wake up. How long did it take to get back from the Spirit World, anyway? Surely it was just a matter of opening your eyes? It wasn't like she had to take a shuttle or something!

His mother pulled him out of the quiet room for dinner in the hospital cafeteria.

"The doctor says he's run out of tests," she told Jase wearily. "And he still has no idea why she isn't waking up. He's given her the strongest stimulant he's willing to use, until her case becomes desperate. And it's not desperate yet," she added, with determined optimism. "In fact, he's recommending we simply wait a few days and see if she wakes up naturally."

She should have awakened, naturally, several hours ago. If Otter Woman had kept her word. Or maybe it did take a while to get back from the Spirit World. Jase might have asked his grandfather, but he was afraid to hear the answer.

"What does Dad think?"

"He thinks it's time to call in an expert, and he's got a couple of assistants working late to compile information on the leading specialists in comas and neurological disorders. He'll have their files on his desk tomorrow morning, but it might take a while to get your grandmother in to see one of them, since her case isn't an emergency."

"And what does Grandfather want to do? Doesn't he have final say on Gima's treatment?"

"He does, and he agrees with the doctor. In fact, he plans to rent a van and drive your grandmother home tomorrow. There's a registered nurse in the village who can take care of her. Your grandfather says she'll return from her journey in her own good time, and wake up in her own bed when she does."

"I hope he didn't say that in Dad's hearing."

Jase was glad he'd spent most of the day in his grandmother's room.

"No, I've managed to keep them apart for the moment," his mother said. "And I'm going to keep doing it until your father has chosen a specialist, and it's time to send her for treatment. That will take days, maybe as much as a week. I think, I hope, that if she hasn't awakened by then your grandfather will be ready to OK more treatment. If he doesn't"—her lips tightened—"your father knows good custody lawyers."

Jase's jaw dropped. "He'd sue for the right to take Gima's treatment decisions out of Gramps' hands? He'll never forgive him for that! Never. And I couldn't blame him!"

"You father knows that. But he can't just stand around and watch Gima die."

"You said she wasn't dying. Her vital signs are stable, and her brain is fine!" His voice rose, and the people seated nearby looked at him with pity in their eyes.

"She's all right, for now," his mother said. "With any luck, please God, she'll wake up soon and be just fine. But if she doesn't . . . Your father will have to act, Jase. He doesn't have a choice."

Jase knew exactly how that felt. "Do you want me to drive you home? I need to get some sleep."

Urgently.

His mother looked tempted, but she shook her head. "Your grandfather plans to sleep tonight, since he'll be driving all day tomorrow, and your father's sitting up with Gima. I'll stay."

Jase wanted to stay too, but he didn't dare. He drove home, downed some of his father's pills, and fell into sleep as if he'd jumped off a cliff.

He woke in the morning, with no memory of having dreamed at all.

Otter Woman was avoiding him.

Bitch.

Jase dug into the pantry till he found his mother's ragbag, and hung strips of every bright color he could find off the balcony railing. Surely such a clear emergency signal would bring Raven to see what was wrong, no matter how angry she was.

He was still trying to think of a way to explain this display when his parents came in.

His grandmother's condition was unchanged. Before they left the hospital, they'd seen her loaded into the back of his grandfather's rental van and strapped in for the drive, with monitoring equipment hooked up and running.

His mother was gray with exhaustion, but on his father's face Jase saw a determination that frightened him more than grief.

Files that contained information on specialists would be

on his desk today. He'd be in touch with one of them, making an appointment for Gima before nightfall, because he was going to save his mother—and he didn't care what got wrecked along the way.

They went to bed without even glancing at the bright fringe that rimmed the deck.

o   o   o

When his parents woke in the late afternoon, Jase told his mother that the bright cloth was an experiment to see if more rufous hummingbirds could be lured to a feeder. The project was due at the end of the week, he said, so he had to start now. He didn't have anything else to do, so he might as well finish his homework.

His father, in a hurry to reach his office, didn't even ask.

The rest of the day dragged past. His grandfather didn't call to say his wife had awakened. Raven didn't knock on his door to ask why Jase was shouting for help.

Just after eight, his grandfather finally appeared on the house com screen to let them know he was home and had put Gima to bed. She was still sleeping, but the nurse was looking after her body, and her spirit would return when it was ready.

Jase might have found that reassuring, if the com screen hadn't revealed the haunting fear in the old man's eyes.

He took his sleeping pills, went to bed, and dreamed he was looking frantically for something he had to find. His heart was pounding and sweat slicked his body, but the vital thing continued to elude him. He bruised his fingers turning over rocks, and scraped his chest sliding down a tree he'd climbed for some reason that wasn't quite clear.

In the morning, there were no marks on his skin—a normal nightmare, with a normal cause.

Jase lurked near the household com while his mother called his grandfather, but he already knew the result—his grandmother's body was still in a coma, because her spirit was trapped in another world.

Otter Woman had broken her promise.

And Raven hadn't turned up either, which she would, surely she would, if she were free.

They weren't coming back from the Spirit World, either of them. Not unless someone went to get them.

It was time to learn about his heritage.

CHAPTER 11

JASE STARTED ON THE NET. It felt like an odd place to research how to enter the Spirit World, but Raven would call that "human knowledge," and the net was where human knowledge was stored and accessed.

Though when it came to entering interdimensional interfaces, human knowledge was pretty scant. The closest Jase came was an article in a folklore journal about hills as portals, which referenced the Celtic fairy mounds, the cavernous Greek underworld, and "a number of stone piles in Alaska and Canada that were said to be portals to the Spirit World." Which would be fine, if any source had mentioned where those piles were or how you used them.

Jase decided to focus in, and searched for references to Ananuts entering the Spirit World. All he learned was that Ananut shamans painted the path to the Spirit World on the bodies of the dead and dying to guide them there. And much as he wanted to get into the Spirit World, he didn't want to die for it.

Jase thought about calling his grandfather then. The old man had a book of all the paths that could be painted on a body to guide the spirit. He'd painted the pattern for *child to adult* onto Jase for his coming-of-age ceremony, when he turned thirteen. The colorful swirls of red, blue, and green had tickled going on, itched as they dried, and melted in vivid smears in the steam bath after the ceremony.

Would his grandfather allow him to go adventuring in the Spirit World, which had already claimed his wife?

That was another question that Jase preferred not to have answered, but his vague plan was taking shape. It was risky, challenging the enemies who held his grandmother prisoner. But as far as he could see, he wasn't risking anything he hadn't already lost.

He searched some more, and found a site that offered pictures of the Ananuts' painted paths. The one for coming of age (male) looked pretty much like his vague memory of the pattern his grandfather had painted on him, so Jase printed out a copy of the death path. The text made it clear that, despite the name, it was really the path to the Spirit World. And even if it was usually painted on the dead, it didn't say you *had* to die to use it.

o   o   o

It was nine thirty when he knocked on the door in Georg's dorm, and roused him out of a sound sleep.

"For the good God's sake, do you know what time it is?"

Jase averted his eyes from Georg's hairy chest. "It's almost ten. It'll be noon in a few hours."

"Yes, but I don't have classes till three. I remember you. You're Manny's cousin's friend, with that most strange medicine bag. I haven't found a buyer yet, but this man who studies fossil plants has expressed some—"

"I don't want to sell it." Jase's blood ran cold at the thought.

It might have been sold if he'd waited a few more days. "I need to have all that dust back. Now."

Georg scratched his chest, frowning. "I don't know. Your friend, I think he wants the money."

"It's not his dust," Jase said. "And it's not yours, either. It's mine, and I want it back."

Georg eyed him curiously. "Your friend seemed to think he had some share in it."

Jase ungritted his teeth. "Call him. You can ask him yourself."

He could always pay Ferd back, if necessary.

It took only a few minutes before Ferd's face appeared on the com screen in Georg's dorm room.

"Hey there. Have you finally found a buy . . . Bro! I heard about your grandmother. I'm sorry. That's such a—"

"Ferd," Jase interrupted. "I need the dust. Now. Tell Georg to give it to me, OK?"

Ferd's eyes widened, but he came through. "Hey, if you need it, it's yours. You know that."

"I put a lot of time into advertising this sample," Georg said. "Not to speak of analyzing it in the first place."

"Don't worry about that," Ferd told him. "Manny will make it up to you."

Georg grimaced. "Does Manny know this?"

"Not yet," said Ferd. "But he will when I tell him. I'll square it with him later, if I have to."

Jase's eyes stung. Ferd always came through.

"I can pay a bit for your time," he told Georg. "Would you take fifty dollars?"

Georg had bargained him up to eighty by the time they

reached the lab, and he handed over all that was left of the sample—perhaps a tablespoon of grainy dirt.

"But for a sample, for the microscanner, this is a great plenty, yes?"

"Yes." Jase's hand closed over the glass vial. "It's enough."

o   o   o

Raven had said he could reach the sea ley anywhere along the southern coast, but that might not include Anchorage, and Jase didn't dare waste any of his small supply of dust trying to heal the wrong place. He needed to rent a boat and get out into the Sound, and the closest place for that was Seward. Halfway there he stopped at a flash charge station and purchased a late breakfast, a small bottle of nonprescription sleeping pills, and a black marker. The washable kind, made for kids, since he didn't want to be wearing death paint into the next week.

o   o   o

The road down the Kenai Peninsula was made for the Tesla's tires. Jase pulled into the small harbor town shortly after noon. It was drizzling, as it often was on the coast, but too lightly to discourage the tourists. The quaint old shops around the harbor and the Alaska Sealife Center made Seward a prime tourist destination—which also meant Jase could rent the kind of boat he needed.

"You sure you want a bubblehead?"

The clerk at the boat rental counter glanced from Jase's Native features to the Tesla and back again. "I could fix you up with a real boat. One that can crank on some speed."

Jase had encountered that kind of thing so often he no

longer felt compelled to explain that not all Alaska Natives could handle boats.

"Just a bubblehead," he repeated. "That's all I need."

The old joke was that after the bubblehead's designer had reeled off the long list of its safety features to a crowd of rental boatyard owners, he'd finished by proclaiming that this boat was absolutely idiot proof!

Yeah? an old boatman had replied. *Well, that don't make it* tourist *proof.*

They'd been named for the plastic shields that sprang up around the cab in an emergency, and the boat's ability to right itself even if it turned upside down. But bubbleheads were not only unsinkable, their computerized brains kept them clear of other boats, dangerous currents and tides, and any storms the weather satellites were tracking.

All the passenger had to do was pick a destination and the bubblehead would take you there. And if you picked a destination that was dangerous, in restricted waters, or in the middle of dry land, the boat politely told you it couldn't go there and explained why.

Jase rented a two-seater, since he had no need for anything larger and even this small boat cost a full car payment. He climbed over the high side and into a bucket seat not unlike the Tesla's. Since it was raining, he ordered the plastic canopy up.

"Would you like to input a *Destination*?" the mechanized voice asked. "Or if you wish to describe what you're looking for, I can suggest *Options*?"

"Options," Jase told it. "I'm looking for . . ." *Ley* wouldn't be on the list of words it was programmed to recognize. "Ocean. Scenery. Beauty. Shore. Picnic."

After he'd healed the ley, he'd need to get to shore as quickly as possible. He thought it would take them a while to get here, but he wanted to be well concealed by the time they did.

A map screen extruded from the control panel in front of him, and two dozen red dots began to blink, showing the locations that matched his criteria.

There was a lot of beautiful scenery on the Alaskan coast. If he hadn't added a need to picnic on the shore the whole map would probably be alight. As it was . . .

Jase almost chose the nearest dot that was out of the bay and in the Sound itself, but that was a major boat lane. He needed someplace less crowded — if nothing else, knowing that people in other boats were wondering what he was doing would make him too self-conscious to heal.

That took anyplace near the glacier out of the running — too many tourists.

He finally chose a dot somewhat distant from the others, though it was farther than he'd prefer. But the coastline near it looked accessible, and it was out of the main tourist and shipping routes.

"Excellent choice!" the boat enthused when Jase punched the dot for his destination. "Under current wind and tidal conditions we should reach that point in one hour and twenty-two minutes."

It whirred out of the slip as it spoke, and turned toward the bay's mouth. Jase settled back and prepared to exercise patience. The only complaint tourists had about the bubblehead was that if you told it to go faster it said *Yes sir,* and hummed right along at the same speed it was going before. The boats chose their speed with safety as the first priority, and the fact that most of them were rented by the hour as the second.

They were safe, smart, and reliable—but they didn't go fast.

Besides, Jase figured he could use the extra time to work on the weakest part of his plan—healing the sea.

Raven might have said that he was healing the ley through the sea, but that was too abstract for Jase. And working with dust that hadn't been bound to him or his car, he needed all the reality he could get.

This dust still held the magic that old shaman, Atahalne, had created. It should be able to heal . . . if Jase could do his part.

No Raven to talk him through it this time. No empathy with the sea at all. Most of the tourists on the ferries Jase had taken went out onto the deck to breathe the air, and look at waves and things. Jase had always joined the seasoned commuters, who sat in the center of the cabin and worked or read or watched something on their pods.

The sea was just water as far as he was concerned—water that sometimes heaved up and down, till his inner ear twisted his stomach into heaving chaos.

At least the chop, even after he'd emerged from the bay, was light today. And another thing bubbleheads were good at was adjusting their angle to the waves, to decrease the motion as much as possible. Though it was still beginning to go up and . . . *Don't think about that!*

Sea person he wasn't—but he wasn't a forest person either, and he'd healed the taiga. Could he find that sense of life, of energy, that he'd felt in the taiga here in the sea?

But the trees in the taiga, everything in that icy bog, had been passionately alive. The sea wasn't. Was it?

He'd never find out sitting in a bubble.

They were out of the bay now, running down the coast. Rain still pattered on the plastic shield, but the temp gauge told him it wasn't too cold outside. And it wasn't as if his boat was moving fast enough to generate much wind.

"Top down," Jase ordered, and the shell slid smoothly into the hull.

The rain was cold, but after the stuffy heat of the bubble the air was amazingly fresh. No doubt he had to experience the sea in order to heal it, so Jase shrugged deeper into his jacket and prepared to endure.

After the first few minutes it wasn't that bad. Yes, his face got wet and he had to keep wiping water out of his eyes, but without the rain-streaked plastic blurring his vision, trees and rocks loomed through the mist that shrouded the shore like a high-priced Asian watercolor.

The boat's electric motor was so quiet Jase could hear the silence—an active absence of sound that showcased the gurgle of the waves and the screeching cry of a gull. Eventually his course took him behind the spur of land at the west end of the bay, and the chop eased.

He passed a raft of sea otters—they hung around most of the coastline looking cute for the tourists. With Otter Woman in mind, Jase didn't find them all that cute. But they gazed back at him with a sober curiosity that didn't seem unfriendly.

Even this far from the glacier, he passed bits of sea ice, their jagged edges sculpted into sharp points and smooth curves by sun and water. He could see the green-white curves beneath the surface as well, because the sea was clear as glass.

A soft ripple welled in front of the bow, and flowed into a long V behind the boat. Jase pulled down his hood and let the drizzle soak into his hair—wet, like the sea. He stretched down to dip his hand in the water and found it colder than the rain.

When he touched his fingers to his tongue he tasted salt, but not as intensely as he'd expected.

What he was experiencing now wasn't the sea—this was the air above the sea. But if he had to immerse himself in the sea in order to heal it, his plan was in trouble. Water that cold could kill in minutes. No way was he—

"Destination reached." The bubblehead came to a stop.

The shore was farther than it had looked on the map, but the beach was broad and sandy, and the tree-clad hills were low enough not to trap him in the open. Being at sea was the point, after all. Jase was beginning to get a sense of it too. Not alive, not like the taiga had been, but it held a subtle energy that was utterly different. Clear and cold and empty, though Jase knew it held all kinds of life. Its currents swept the globe, charging the climate and the atmosphere, as much a part of the world as the rock plates he lived on.

Was this enough? This clean sweep of energy that felt so tenuous he wasn't even sure if he was sensing something, or just imagining it. And what did you say to heal the sea?

He wasn't really here to heal the sea, anyway, and he had a feeling magic wouldn't work with lies.

I hope this works was no longer in his heart.

What was?

Gima. He was here to heal, not the sea, but his grand-mother, and the injury to her that was tearing his family apart. He wanted to heal all the people he loved. Why not throw the sea into that mix?

Jase pulled the vial from his pocket.

"I want to heal," he said. Truth welled like blood into the

words. "I want to heal Gima, and my father and grandfather, and everything that hurts, that isn't right like it should be. I want you to be well. Be well," he whispered, to his grandmother, and the sea, and all the world—to anything that hurt wherever these waters might reach.

He took a pinch of dust and cast it into the sea.

He was braced this time for the cold sweep of power, so it didn't knock him off his seat. Jase had just released his grip on the side of the boat when the water surged beneath it, heaving the bubblehead up like an express elevator.

"Whoa!"

The bubblehead slithered down the side of the swell, so steeply tilted that for a moment Jase thought it would overturn.

The bubblehead evidently thought so too. The plastic top shot out, bruising his fingers before it closed over his head—which Jase regretted, as the boat bobbed queasily in the choppy aftermath.

The wave that had thrown him skyward was rolling toward shore—there'd better not be any houses on that beach, or they'd be swamped!

But even as he watched, the swell slumped and flattened. By the time it reached the beach it was just a slightly taller breaker, tumbling up the sand.

"Overturning the craft is not recommended," the boat's computer told him sternly.

"I hear you! Top down," Jase added. "And take me to the shore. Quickly."

It didn't move quickly, but it wasn't long before the incoming waves seized the bubblehead and started pushing it toward the shore. The receding waves tried to pull it back, but the motor fought them, and within moments Jase heard sand grate under the hull.

He climbed out, ignoring the cold water sloshing into his shoes, grateful to be on land again. All this motion was affecting his stomach.

The bubblehead was heavier than he'd expected, but Jase put his back into it and dragged the small craft up the beach well past the tide line.

He typed a message on the com screen, and set it to blinking so they couldn't miss it. Then he scrambled up the small bluff and into the trees.

The hills that had looked so low and gentle from out at sea were a lot rougher when he tried to climb them, but the thick tangle of spruce and scrub suited his purpose.

Jase found a thicket so dense he didn't think he could be seen from the beach or the sky, not even by something looking through an eagle's eyes, and settled in to wait. And wait.

Almost twenty minutes later, when his butt was growing cold and numb from the hard ground, an eagle swooped out of the hills and began to circle over the sea where Jase had healed it.

Jase froze, trying not even to breathe as it looped a few more times, then flew to the beach and perched on the bubblehead's side.

A hunter must watch with his eyes alone, his grandfather had told him, long ago. *Don't turn your head to follow its movement. Ease your breathing. And stop wiggling!*

Now Jase was old enough to take that advice. Only his eyes moved to track the sleek brown shape that trundled out of the surf and up the beach.

She changed as she came, the short legs lengthening, the furry body bulging and broadening as the otter's torso lifted upright. It was an old woman who walked the last few steps to the bubblehead, giving it the barest glance before she lifted her gaze to the hillside.

Looking for him.

Jase didn't even dare to close his eyes. Otter Woman hadn't been able to sense the pouch when she'd been in his bedroom, and the tiny bit of dust he had now was much less than that. Still, Jase had to suppress a gasp of relief when her gaze passed over his hiding place.

She turned to the eagle and said something Jase couldn't hear, and the bird hopped down and began to shift.

A swarm of brown dots flew out of the woods to the west and buzzed around the boat—bees, Jase thought, though he was too far off to be certain. The dots circled into a whirling column, tighter and tighter, till the buzzing mob merged into the shape of a man.

As the two faces solidified, the hair on the back of Jase's neck rose. They looked about ten years older than they had when they'd caught Jase in the parking lot, but the eagle was the wide receiver and the bees were the linebacker. He was also the man Jase had thought might be an undercover cop, though he'd looked older then than he did now. Of course, a shapeshifter could probably be any age he chose. Was he also the swarm of bees that had attacked Jase's car on the way home?

Otter Woman had ignored these riveting metamorphoses and was reading Jase's note. It didn't take her long.

If you kill her, I'll heal the air and finish it.

Jase didn't think it was all that complicated, but the three shifters discussed it for a long time. He could tell they were arguing, but not what it was about. Otter Woman did seem to be in charge, but sometimes she listened to the eagle man. They didn't look like high school football players now.

And it was just as well Jase had chosen a beach away from the tourist routes—Alaska wasn't a popular choice for nudists, and a boat captain who depended on family business might have complained to the authorities. The transmitter on the boat, rented on his charge account, would tell them exactly who had been on that beach at this time.

Jase was beginning to get impatient when Otter Woman made a sharp gesture, evidently settling something, and then turned and walked down the beach into the sea. She started to change shortly after she reached the waves, but Jase kept his eyes on the man who was melting and morphing back into an eagle.

He'd never be able to keep track of an otter in the ocean, but he could see the direction an eagle flew.

The man obliged him by taking off in a straight line, west and a bit north.

Jase wished he dared take out his com pod, but the bee man lingered, running his gaze over the tree-clad hillside.

If you hold still you'll be invisible. He could all but hear his grandfather's voice. *Animals see motion more easily than anything else.*

Eventually the man stopped looking, and his shape fragmented into bees once more. But instead of flying off, the swarm spread out and settled around the bubblehead. Jase had read that insects didn't have much distance vision, so he allowed himself to grin.

He knew Otter Woman didn't think much of human intelligence—in fact, he was counting on that. But this trap was so blatant it was almost insulting.

And none of the shifters he'd met had struck him as patient people, either.

Jase settled in to wait him out. The drizzle had stopped, and his rain gear was keeping him warm. Time to draw on his heritage, and channel his inner hunter. Because he knew what he was hunting, and the man on the beach didn't. Bee man would give up before he did.

Jase hung on to that thought and channeled his inner hunter for the better part of an hour, while his butt began to ache and his legs went numb. If he moved around he was sure to be seen, so he hung on to his heritage and waited some more.

After most of another hour had passed Jase was cursing his heritage, and Raven, who'd gotten him into this, and his own stupid half-assed plan. Only the memory of Gima, lying against the hospital pillows with her eyes sealed shut, kept him there.

The sun was breaking through the overcast when the swarm finally lifted, coalesced, and flew off in the same direction the eagle had taken.

It occurred to Jase that Bee Man might have left a few bits of himself, to keep watch and sound an alarm, but Jase had to move now. He stretched out his legs, swearing as cramped muscles screamed, and crawled out of the thicket. Then he pulled out his com pod, centered the GPS app on north, and drew a line across the screen in the direction his enemies had gone. Once he had the line locked, he brought up a map beneath it.

One name leaped out at him, but Alaska Natives had settled all over the state. Just because there was a town there now didn't mean that was the place he was looking for.

There was an easy way to find out. Jase opened a new window and switched the function to call.

"Gramps? Is there one of those rock piles that opens to the Spirit World somewhere along this line?" He dragged the map to the place he wanted it to appear on his grandfather's screen as he spoke.

"What?" Jase had never seen his grandfather look so startled. "Why do you—"

"Just humor me," Jase said. "Are any of those rock-pile spirit places on this line?"

His grandfather looked down. "Yes, in fact. There's a spirit portal west of Whittier, just past the ruins. There's an Olmaat rock on the beach below it, too. A very sacred site."

"What's an Olmaat rock?"

"Why do you care? Aren't you going to ask how your grandmother is?"

"If she'd waked up, Mom would have contacted me," Jase said. The furious grief in the old man's eyes was unbearable. "How is she?"

"Gone," said his grandfather.

Jase's heart froze, then began to beat harder. "You don't mean . . ."

"No, she's not dead, but her spirit's still gone off somewhere. And I don't understand why she's not coming back."

Jase had never heard his grandfather admit there was anything he didn't understand.

"I don't know what else to do." The old man's controlled expression began to crack. "I swear, if she doesn't wake soon I'll have to try your father's way. But with her spirit wandering, I'm afraid that might do her more harm than good, and I don't know . . ." His grandfather's voice husked into silence, and he cleared his throat.

Jase's own throat was too tight for speech.

"Why are you asking about the sacred sites?" the old man went on. "There's nothing I could do for her there that I can't do here."

"I . . ." He could hardly tell his grandfather he was wrong about that. "Thanks, Gramps. I'll talk to you later. Keep Gima safe. Keep watch on her."

His grandfather frowned, and was opening his mouth to ask another question when Jase cut the com. He had no answers, and it would be too cruel to raise his grandfather's hopes and then fail.

He couldn't fail.

CHAPTER 12

IT WAS JUST AFTER FOUR when the bubblehead returned Jase to the boat dock, and a five-hour drive from Seward to Whittier. Jase thought about checking in at home, but there was too much risk that his parents would try to keep him there. Instead he stopped at a restaurant in Anchorage for dinner, and then commed home and left a message that he'd decided to stay with Gramps for a while, and see if he could help him out.

His mother would find out Gramps hadn't agreed to that the next time she called for an update on Gima's condition, but she and his grandfather would both think that Jase had decided to show up at the door and then talk his way in.

By the time they realized he hadn't arrived, Jase hoped to be finished. And after they commed to tell him Gima was awake, it wouldn't matter where he went.

Jase drove straight from Anchorage, through the tunnel and down into Whittier.

He'd never learned why some fool had constructed the huge apartment buildings to the west of town, or why they'd been abandoned. Perhaps they'd been damaged in one of the earthquakes that periodically shook the coast. Perhaps it was simply that no one wanted to live in Whittier.

The small town held only a cannery, and the harbor where

the glacier cruises and the ferry docked. The basic setup wasn't so different from many coastal towns, but in Whittier the mountains loomed over the harbor, and the ruins of the great apartment complex shadowed everything with an air of grim decay.

It was, of course, drizzling.

There were still roads out to the empty apartments and Jase drove there, parking the Tesla as far from the crumbling buildings as he could. He pulled his rain jacket out of the trunk, and after a moment's hesitation strapped a canteen and belt over it. His grandfather had said there was an Olmaat rock on the beach below the spirit gate, so Jase set off walking along the shoreline, planning to find the Olmaat rock and then hike up. His grandfather's version of "just past the ruins" could be anything up to a mile, in Jase's experience, but the wet sand was firm under his gel-soles—easy walking. It was past ten now, and the low sun peeked under the cloud cover in scattered patches.

Jase hoped he'd recognize the Olmaat rock when he saw it. He hoped the spirit portal wouldn't be hidden too deeply in the trees. He hoped that at least one of his ideas for using it would work—if he couldn't enter the Spirit World, sooner or later his grandmother's body would die.

And maybe his world if Raven was right about the tree plague, but that was a battle for the future, for other people to fight. Jase's job was to get his grandmother back. After that, if he could, he'd finish healing the ley and be done with it. Before other people he loved got hurt, because of him.

He needn't have worried about recognizing the Olmaat rock. Less than a quarter mile from the ruins, it stood out starkly against the chalky bluff, a misplaced chunk of dark gray stone that had probably been dumped by some ancient glacier. There was no other rock of that color, no other large rocks nearby. Jase could see why the first people who'd lived and fished off this shore had noticed it, and carved their sym- bols onto its surface.

But as he drew near, something about the rock began to tickle that other sense, the new one that had touched the life in the taiga and the cold clear energy of the sea.

There was a wrongness about the Olmaat rock, a darkness that made the back of Jase's neck prickle—which was absurd. It was nothing but a big chunk of stone.

Jase couldn't even read ancient Ananut symbols, and this had been some other tribe's territory—but he'd bet those enig- matic lines and curves were signs of warning.

Keeping an eye on the dark rock—ridiculous! What did he think it was going to do?—Jase looked for a way up the bluff. It was only thirty or forty feet high, but it was too steep to climb and looked slippery.

A handful of yards beyond the rock Jase found a path up the bluff. It was only a narrow rim of beaten earth winding up the slope, but that was all the ancient people would have needed. Their modern descendants, at least the kind who reg- ularly visited sacred sites, would probably make a fetish of us- ing the ancient paths too.

"You could at least have put up a railing," Jase grumbled as he started up the track. It wasn't as bad as he'd expected. The drizzle was beginning to lift, the packed earth was sticky under his shoes, not slippery, and the path was wider than it looked from below.

As long as he didn't look down.

When he neared the top, the trail turned into a cleft in the bluff that took him up the rest of the way. From the cliff's edge Jase looked out over the bay. More open, far more inviting than Whittier itself, the bay was rimmed by the same kind of tree-clad slopes that rose behind him. Glaciers threaded through some of the gaps between those hills, flowing down to the quiet water.

The clouds were still too low for Jase to see the top of the higher mountains, but what he could see was beautiful.

Jase turned and took the path inland. The portal, when he reached it, was almost as unmistakable as the Olmaat rock: a pile of small boulders more than twice Jase's height.

The stones that formed it were much the same color as the Olmaat rock, but they didn't feel the same. Reaching out clumsily with that tenuous, other sense, Jase didn't pick up anything except a hint of . . . other? travel? difference?

Whatever it was, it didn't bother him the way the Olmaat rock did. Jase followed the path around the piled stones, in case there was an actual opening you could walk through and find yourself in the Spirit World.

There wasn't.

That didn't surprise him, but he'd have felt really stupid if he'd spent half the night trying other ways and then walked to the other side and found a door.

Now for the hard way.

The rain had stopped while he explored the rock pile, leaving the air so fresh it almost hurt to breathe. Jase pulled out his print of the death path and studied the complex stripes and swirls. This might be easier with a mirror, but he didn't have one. And he had a hunch that magic worked more off the intent of the user than precise artwork, anyway.

He stripped off his rain jacket, then his shirt, flinching as cold air met warm skin. He pulled out the black marker and started with the deep V under the hollow between his collarbones, which seemed to center the whole design. After a while his hand grew more confident, and he began to pick up on patterns, as he sometimes did in the curving body of a well-designed car. The slanting lines over the ribs drew down to the center, not up and out. And that spiral down the middle of his torso, ending at his navel, was supposed to pull him not only down, but in.

In and down. Every black mark on his body confirmed that theme. By the time Jase was finished drawing he was almost sure his next idea wouldn't work either, but it would be both faster and easier if it did.

He waited a few minutes for the marks to dry, then put his shirt and jacket back on. He found a flat face on the rock pile, where he'd have put an invisible door if he'd been designing it, took a deep breath and closed his eyes.

"I believe I can walk through," he said firmly. "I believe I can walk right through these rocks and into the Spirit World. I believe."

Mustering all the conviction he could—and having his eyes shut helped, when it came to not believing in solid rock—Jase walked forward as if the stone pile wasn't even there.

He bruised his toe, his knee, and his knuckles when he threw out a hand to catch himself.

"Carp." One of the knuckles bled. Jase licked it, and resigned himself to entering the Spirit World the hard way.

The design on his chest spelled out the answer. Down, and in, and darkness.

Jase found a place where he could sit with his back against the rocks and pulled out the sleeping pills. He was so tired, if he'd been in a warm bed, he probably wouldn't have needed them. Leaning on a rain-wet pile of rocks, he took three.

Remembering what had happened before, he pulled off his belt and strapped his ankles together. If his real-world body should happen to start moving without his direction, he didn't want it to go stumbling off a cliff. Hopefully the belt would prevent that.

Jase closed his eyes and tried to get comfortable. Eventually a mild dizziness swept over him, his muscles relaxed, and the darkness pulled him down.

Jase opened his eyes in the Spirit World.

It was the first time he'd had a chance to examine the place, without being distracted by arguing with Otter Woman or running for his life. It looked much like the real world, though the rock pile was more luminous than it should be in the Arctic twilight, and the rain that had happened so recently in his world . . . hadn't.

At least this world was warmer. Jase set off, walking away from the bluffs. He couldn't feel his real body now. If he didn't try to connect with it, it should stay where he'd left it. And if he was right about how things worked in dreams, it didn't matter what direction he went.

He concentrated on Gima, on his need to find her, to see her again. He passed through glades and meadows thinking about his grandmother. Jase was concentrating so hard that he'd walked past the pond before he realized that the frogs weren't making their usual kid's-horn honk, but instead croaking, "Hey boy. Heeey boy."

Frog People was one of Raven's allies. Raven's enemies could assume any shape they chose. On the other hand, Jase needed all the help he could get. He turned and waded through the long grass to the edge of the pond. He didn't have to wait long.

Frogs swam from every corner of the marsh; their heads emerged to make rippling circles in the water for a moment, before they ducked below the surface once more. They climbed on top of each other, in a squirming pile of green-brown skin and thrashing legs, and then began to melt and merge, not into human form, but into a giant frog. A human face emerged, like a mask pasted onto a wide, neckless head.

The bulging eyes opened and looked Jase over, and an expression of purely human skepticism brought the face to life.

"So you're Raven's boy. You don't look like much."

Jase didn't care what he looked like.

"How do I know you're not one of Raven's enemies, assuming a frog shape?"

Frog People considered this. "You don't. And I gotta say, there's more chance of that now than there was at first. Used to be, everyone laughed when Raven said she could get humans to heal the ley. Now that ley's flowing clear and clean and bright, almost to the node! One more healing would do it!"

The frog wiggled with enthusiasm, settling its feet and narrow rump deeper into the mud. "I tell you, the neutrals are looking at this different now. They're saying if humans can fix the problem, why not let 'em? And some of the others, they're beginning to drift into the neutral camp. 'Course, that only makes the enemies who're left more stubborn. More desperate too. The girl was bad enough, but when that pouch was passed to you they said that was the end of it. That you could never use it, and Raven had failed, and we could all forget the matter. You proved 'em wrong. Made fools of them. They won't forget."

"Great," said Jase. Unforgiving, humiliated enemies were just what he needed. "How do I get my grandmother out of here? I can't go back to healing the ley until I do."

Frog People's shoulders weren't designed to shrug, but they slid forward and back. "I don't know how you get her out, but I know how they're keeping her here. When Raven bound the catalyst to you, she also, inadvertent like, bound the people you're linked to into that magic. That link, to magic they control, is what Otter Woman and the others are using to hold her."

Dark green patches began to bloom on the skin of the human face, and Jase realized he didn't have much time.

"How do I break that link?"

"Can't." The bulbous eyes blinked, and for a moment Jase thought he saw compassion in them. "You carry bits of her in every cell of your body. Even if you didn't, and you could stop loving her, you can't keep her from loving you. With the pouch in their control, that's enough for them to bind her spirit."

A small frog pulled itself out of the giant frog's back as if extracting itself from a sticky mold. It wiggled the last webbed foot free and plopped into the water.

Jase couldn't afford to be distracted. "What if I get the pouch back? If I control the dust, can I free her then?"

"Sure. Get that pouch into your hands, she'll go scooting right out of here."

More frogs were peeling away. He was running out of time.

"Where's the pouch?" Jase asked urgently. "How do I get it?"

"No idea. Otter Woman and her frien's hid it, and if they're telling anyone where it is, they're not tellin' me."

Frog People settled deeper into the pond as he disintegrated. "But it's hiddun in your worl'. You'll likely haffa free its magic here to fin' it there. I wisssh oo . . ."

His face dissolved into a writhing mass of frogs before he finished, and Jase suppressed a grimace as he stepped away.

If that had been one of Raven's enemies, disguising himself as Frog People, wouldn't he have given Jase more "helpful" information than that? Something that would help him right off a cliff, instead of setting him to wander in circles.

Whether that was Frog People or not, one thing he'd said was true. Otter Woman had hidden the pouch, so she'd know where it was. And Otter Woman held Gima, so she'd know where his grandmother was and how to free her. Which meant the next logical step was for Jase to find Otter Woman, and see if he could learn anything from her.

He set off walking again, concentrating on Otter Woman and his grandmother. Though after what felt like hours of aimless wandering, he began to doubt that his finding-people-in-dreams-by-thinking-about-them theory was working as well as he'd hoped.

Jase pulled the canteen off his belt—which was still holding up his pants, here in this world—drank, then took out his com pod to check the time. When he thumbed it on, it turned into a giant beetle that wiggled its long antennae and bit his hand.

"Ow!" Jase shook it off, and watched it buzz away into the distance. This wasn't his world. He'd do well to remember that. In fact, looking more closely, he saw that the filaments he'd taken for natural fiber in the center of the flowers to the right of his path were really a nest of fishhooks. The kind that had stuck in his fingers, and once hooked painfully through the top of his ear when his grandfather tried to teach him to fish.

Well, that was one direction he wouldn't be go—

Jase stopped and stared at the hook-flowers. All of them grew on one side of the path, forming a barrier that herded him in the direction they wanted him to go. Just like the bramble patch had turned him onto this path. And that rock fall had kept him from climbing the slope, when he'd wanted to go up and look at the terrain.

Jase turned and walked directly into the flowers. He had to move slowly to keep the hooks from digging into his clothing, and despite his care, his fingers were pricked raw with extracting them by the time he came out of the flowers . . . and plunged into woods that grew so thickly he had to wade through them as if he were swimming.

Jase wasn't even surprised when he came out of the woods and saw the glacier blocking his path—not the snow-capped sheets of ice they showed on d-vid, but its receding edge. The barren, plowed-up earth and jagged boulders looked like a bomb had been dropped there. He picked his way through the muddy rubble and climbed onto the ice. The places that weren't studded with gravel were as slippery as he'd expected.

He walked across the glacier for a long time, crawling when the footing was too treacherous, with meltwater soaking the knees of his jeans. He prayed no sudden crevasse would open up to swallow him, but the forest on the other side of the massive ice field grew nearer, and nearer. When he slithered down, a clear path awaited him.

Jase didn't even try the path, plunging into the thickest tangle of scrub he could see. When he finally struggled out, rubbing his scratched face and hands, he emerged into a glade. Otter Woman stood at the other side with the two men he'd seen at the beach beside her. At least this time they were clothed. The men's faces were hard, but Jase thought he saw a cruel pleasure in the Bee Man's dark eyes. How could he ever have believed they were kids his own age?

Behind the three of them was a raven in a cage, and Jase's grandmother.

She was smiling widely and Jase started to run forward, but the raven squawked and flapped frantically. The bars were so close it couldn't spread its wings, and when one of them brushed the cage it cringed. But it didn't take its eyes off him, or quit shrieking, until Jase stopped running and approached more cautiously.

He'd never seen his grandmother wearing makeup before. The ancient Ananut painted their bodies only for ceremony. Jase had heard modern Ananut girls joke that they were dedicating themselves to the hunt when they put on lipstick, but he'd never seen it on his grandmother.

"You surprise me, boy," said Otter Woman. "I didn't think you could come here without help."

"I didn't think you'd break your word," said Jase. "So I guess we're both stupid."

Her lips tightened. "Would a human keep his word to a dog? That's all you are to us. That's all you are to Raven, no matter how sweetly she pleasures you."

"Pleasures? We don't . . . I mean, we haven't . . ."

Jase dragged his mind from this conversational track with some difficulty. The last thing he wanted to discuss with Otter Woman was his sex life.

"OK, maybe we aren't worth keeping your word to, but we don't abuse our dogs. We don't keep them prisoner while their bodies weaken, and their families suffer."

Gima nodded, but she said nothing. Looking closely at her bright-colored lips, Jase saw that the smile had been painted on. Under the paint . . . were those stitches, holding her lips shut?

He shuddered, and prayed with all his heart that was just a metaphor produced by his dreaming mind—for there was no doubt his grandmother had been silenced. It might well be a metaphor, because it also looked as if her feet were growing roots into the ground. Gima wasn't here, physically; this was her spirit. And how much of her spirit was her?

Her eyes, at least, were her own. Worried, angry, frightened, but bright with thought, they darted from one of her captors to another. She caught Jase's gaze and reached up with both hands to either side of her neck, then ran her fingers down to close together, as if she was grasping something.

Seeing his fixed gaze, Otter Woman started to turn.

"I have some dust left," Jase said quickly. "I can still heal the final part of the ley. And if I do, the neutrals are going to insist you let Raven finish the job. Since humans have proved we can heal them. Why not let us? And why do you get to keep Raven prisoner? I thought you weren't allowed to interfere, directly."

"I convinced Bear that with you stopped, and the catalyst in my hands, there was no way Raven could win. She vowed to go on fighting, and eventually Bear said, 'Enough.' Between them, the neutrals have the power to overcome any of us."

The eagle man frowned at this, but Otter Woman didn't even glance in his direction. These ageless warriors might look formidable, but Otter Woman was the brains.

"Just because a few of you, under our guidance, did one thing right, that doesn't make up for centuries of spreading poison," she went on. "And as for Raven"—she gestured at the caged bird and grinned nastily—"there are consequences for losing."

"Losing what?" Jase demanded. "If I heal that last piece of the ley, Raven will have won!"

"And you'll spend the next year or so watching your grandmother's empty body die by inches," said Otter Woman. "Is that a trade you're willing to make, young Ananut?"

"No." Jase didn't even have to think about it.

Two tears ran down Gima's face, but her gaze was intent. She put her hands up to her neck once more, ran them down to her breast and clasped something. A necklace? A—

"Then give us the catalyst," Otter Woman said. "All of it, this time. And we'll let your grandmother go."

"We made that deal already," said Jase. "And you broke it. If I give you the remaining dust, I've got no way to enforce the deal. I was stupid enough to take your word once, but not twice. Not without a guarantee. I want Bear to *give his word, to stand surety for you. Then I'll make the deal."*

The old woman's furious hiss sounded more animal than human. "You have no right to dictate to me, boy!"

"You had no right to kidnap my grandmother," Jase snapped back. "I'm not giving up a single speck of dust until I get a contract I can trust!"

"A contract. You're an Ananut, all right."

"Worse than that," Jase told her. "My dad's a lawyer."

She snorted and turned to the bee man. "Get Bear. If he insists on representing the neutrals, he's going to have to get off his fat butt and do it."

Behind Otter Woman, his grandmother was shaking her head, making the sign for the medicine pouch over and over.

"I understand," said Jase, looking directly into her eyes before he turned back to Otter Woman. "I understand there are more of the neutrals than people on your side, and more are moving to Raven's side all the time. Why don't you just let humans heal the leys? If we broke it, why not let us fix it?"

"Because it won't stay fixed! I may not have dealt with your kind as much as Raven has, but the one thing you always are is human. Heedless, savage, careless of what you wreck on the way to what you want."

"Just like you," said Jase. "Killing my grandmother and wrecking my family to win a political fight."

The indifference in her face made his blood run cold. This old woman would let nothing stop her, even if that meant destroying the human race.

"You know," said Jase, "we've gotten wiser in the last

century or so. We try not to wipe out whole species to save ourselves a little inconvenience."

"How adult of you." Otter Woman turned toward a crashing in the brush, and the bee man walked into the clearing, with a grizzly lumbering after him.

Even knowing this was an alien shapeshifter, not a bear, a primal chill ran through Jase's veins at seeing the great beast so close.

"Wha' do you want?" the bear rumbled.

"It's not me who's disturbing you," Otter Woman said. "This human boy demands you give surety for the bargain we're about to make. He doesn't trust me."

"Smart boy," said the bear. "You lie almos' as much as she does." One paw gestured to the captured Raven, who croaked a protest.

"Bal'erdash," the bear continued. "You lie all the time. Jus' not as nazty with it. Make your bargain, human," he added, turning back to Jase. "I'm hungry."

"I promise to turn over all the dust in my possession," Jase said carefully, "if Otter Woman will free my grandmother and Raven. And never interfere in any way, with any of my family, ever again!"

"That's not what you said the first time," Otter Woman objected.

"I'm not an idiot. I'm not going to give up the only leverage I have, just to see you kidnap one of my parents tomorrow."

"Well, I'm not an idiot either. Suppose you've got more of it cached away somewhere? And even if you don't, humans made that dust. What's to stop you from making more?"

"So what if we make more? So what if we healed every ley in creation? That's what you want!"

"A good poin-t." The great bear nodded. "A very good poin'. Why not let them go? See if Raven can finizh it, like she says she can."

"That's what we agreed to when this started!" Otter Woman's face twisted in frustration. "How about a simpler bargain, human? You give me that dust, or I'll turn Bee People loose on your grandmother right now! If her spirit returned to her body mad, or tormented into idiocy, well, after such a prolonged coma no one would be surprised, would they?"

For the first time, the bee man smiled, and Jase's heart flinched. Gima was shaking her head, Don't do it, don't give in.

He turned to Raven. Slowly, reluctantly, the bird nodded.

"She'll do it," the bear confirmed. "Otter's alwayz had a mean streak."

If he didn't agree, she'd hurt Gima. He couldn't allow that. And if Otter Woman refused to let her go . . .

His father was a lawyer.

"If I give you the dust," Jase said, "all the dust I have, all that I know where it is, you, Bear, will keep my grandmother safe? Keep her from being tortured, or harmed in any way?"

The bear considered this. "Eventually, just being kep' from her body will kill her. Humans ain't dezigned to disincorporate for long."

"But you won't let her be hurt," Jase insisted. "She'll be well treated till she's freed?"

"If Otter Woman agrees, I'll enforze it," the bear said.

"And if he hasn't given up all the catalyst he has, with no more stashed away, then I can vent my anger however I wish," said Otter Woman. "That's part of it."

Jase knew the words were meant for him more than Bear. She needn't have bothered—he was already terrified.

"Don' stop him from making more," Bear pointed out. "or you from taking some other perzon he loves."

"I won't try to make more dust," said Jase. "I wouldn't begin to know how, anyway."

"And I won't take another of his relatives. Or friends," the old woman said. "Or anyone he loves. This hostage appears to be sufficient."

Raven croaked.

"And the terms of the original bargain will still be in effec'," Bear confirmed.

Had Raven seen it too?

Bear waited, but Otter Woman had no more terms to add. Jase didn't dare say more, lest she suddenly see the loophole she had missed.

"Done," Bear pronounced. "The boy handz over all the catalyst he controls, and you don' hurt the human woman. And Otter, don' think of trying to. When I enforze a bargain, I enforze it."

"Agreed." Jase pulled the small vial from his pocket and held it out. His hand trembled slightly—he hoped she wouldn't see it.

Otter Woman looked a bit reluctant, but she took the container from him. "Agreed."

Bee People pouted. The caged Raven ruffled her feathers in distress. Jase's grandmother had both hands clasped in front of her chest, as if she was praying . . . or grasping a medicine bag.

"Don't worry, Gima," said Jase. "I'll get you out of this. I promise."

He laid his hand over his chest and slowly closed it. To the watching shapeshifters it would have looked like a gesture that sealed a vow. Jase didn't think even Raven understood.

But his grandmother did.

∘ ∘ ∘

No one tried to stop him as he left the clearing. They probably assumed he was going back to the stone pile, out of the Spirit World. Instead Jase retraced his steps to Frog People's pond, and found that this time the glacier wasn't as slippery, and the flower's thorns weren't as aggressive as they'd been.

And this time, the frogs weren't calling him as he approached. After he'd waited several minutes, a single frog swam up and crawled onto a flat rock.

"Mucked it up, didn't you?" Its voice was the same as the giant frog's, astonishing from such a small creature.

"I didn't have a choice," Jase pointed out. "I couldn't let her hurt my grandmother."

"Yeah, but you gave up the last of the catalyst," the frog complained. "And what did I tell you? I told you to find the medicine bag, not to — "

"I didn't give up the medicine bag," Jase said. "I turned over all the dust I had, all I possessed, all that I knew where it was. I don't control the medicine bag or know where it is.

So I can still use that, if I can find it. You've got to tell me where it is."

"I still don't know," the frog replied. "But if that's the deal you struck . . . I don't know where it is. I don't even know who knows, but Goose Woman might. She hears lots of things that people aren't supposed to tell her. Pillow talk."

"Can you take me to her?" Jase asked. "I'm tired of thrashing around in bogs and brambles."

His feet were tired, his hands were raw, and a meal and a hot bath sounded really good to him. And he hadn't even begun to free his grandmother yet.

The tiny frog eyed him curiously. "I can guide you. But you should know, boy, one of the reasons you're so tired is that there's as much of your body here as there is in your world. What happens to you here will happen to all of you, everywhere."

"All of me? Are there more . . . This is one of those weird, theoretical physics things, isn't it? I hated that class."

"OK," said Frog People. "I'll make it simple. If you die here, you die. Period. No waking up and going home, like your grandma would."

Jase had already figured that out. "I thought Otter Woman and the others were forbidden to kill me. The terms of the original bargain still stand."

"They stand back in your world," Frog People told him. "No one expected you to start wandering around in the interface, so that's what you might call a gray area. Otter Woman doesn't much like gray. She'd probably have killed you when you first turned up, if Bear and some of the others hadn't come down on her about what she tried to do to

Raven's last human. Very direct, that was. If you head out of here like she thinks you will, she'll probably let you go. Once she sees you're not being a good boy . . . You can be hurt here. You can be killed."

His whole body ached already. But his heart hurt worse.

"I'm not leaving till Gima's free," Jase said. "Mr. Hill-yard was right—if you really want something, you're willing to pay for it. Like the taiga does."

The round frog-eyes blinked. "What's wrong with the taiga? It's a great place. A little chilly in winter, but I can adapt to that."

"It is great," Jase agreed. "But it has to burn in order to grow. Take me to Goose Woman."

CHAPTER 13

With the frog clinging to his collar, its voice booming in his ear, navigating the Spirit World proved easier. There were still patches of bog, and berry brambles with long thorns, but his small guide steered him around the worst obstacles. Soon Jase found himself approaching what looked like an old-style bark-covered round house, on the shore of a rippling lake. Jase was pretty sure there were no lakes this size within walking distance of Whittier, but then the leather flap across the doorway lifted and he forgot about Spirit World geography.

The woman who emerged was older than he was, maybe in her midtwenties, with the clearest skin and the warmest dark eyes he'd ever seen. She wore the beaded leathers that had been summer garb for many Alaska Natives before cloth came into their world, but something about the way she wore it proclaimed that she'd just as soon get out of it.

Jase felt his whole body coming alive, before he got within ten feet of her.

The frog on his shoulder shot her a disgusted look.

"Ease up, would you? He's got to ask you some questions, and he needs to be able to think straight."

"He could think afterward." Her voice managed to

be husky and musical at the same time, and a thrill shot through Jase's blood.

"He needs to think now," Frog People said. "Let up, will you?"

Jase struggled to think. It wasn't easy.

"Please." His voice emerged in a croak, and he cleared his throat before going on. "I need some . . . some information. I need to ask you where Otter Woman . . ." His thoughts were dissolving in a sensual haze. "Where Otter Woman hid . . . Please," he whispered. He wasn't entirely certain what he was pleading for.

"You have to choose."

She moved closer, till he'd have sworn he was picking up her scent—spicy, musky, deep. He could have fallen into it.

"Play or talk?" she asked. "You can't have both. I'd rather play."

She licked her lips, making the type of play she had in mind abundantly clear. Jase summoned reserves of will he'd have sworn he didn't possess.

"I'd rather talk." He hoped he didn't have to sound as if he meant it. "Talk, please."

Her sigh was deep enough to lift the leather over her breasts, but that honey-thick allure lessened so suddenly he almost staggered.

If he could bottle what she had he'd make billions—in the nanosecond before it was declared an illegal drug. But whatever it was, once she'd turned it off it was gone. Jase felt nothing more than a natural reaction when the beautiful woman stepped forward and took him in her arms.

Not that his natural reaction wasn't distracting.

"Hey, I chose talk." Unable to believe he was doing this,

he put his hands on her hips and tried to push her away. "Talk!"

"I don't want to be seen talking to you," she murmured, snuggling closer. "So relax."

Relaxed he wasn't, but Jase let her arms slide around him. "Do you know where the medicine pouch is? The one Otter Woman's using to hold my grandmother here?"

Her body was soft against his, but a rising sense of danger cooled his arousal.

"I do know. People tell me things." Amusement rippled in her voice. "Mostly I don't care, but the ley here feels a lot better since Raven's been working on it. I like this part of the world, so this time I listened."

Her lips feathered along his jaw to his ear, and despite the urgency of the moment, Jase forgot how to breathe.

"It's hidden next to the Olmaat's heart," Goose Woman whispered. "Find it, or let it find you, and you've found the pouch. Getting your hands on the pouch, that's another matter, young warrior."

"The Ananut were traders," Jase said huskily.

"Not all of them."

Her smile made it clear that some had been lovers. She pulled back a bit, walking her fingers up his chest in childish flirtation—and for the first time, Jase noticed that she was taller than he was. Remembering some of the classier vids he'd seen, he captured her hand and kissed it.

"So how do I get it?" he murmured. "You mean the pouch is actually inside its body? Not in a vest pocket or something?"

"Inside its body," she confirmed. "The only way to get it is to kill the Olmaat. Good luck with that."

She gave him a final soft kiss, turned, and went back into her round house. Leaving Jase torn between shuddering horror and delight.

"Wow," he told the frog. "I mean . . . Well, wow."

"You got what you came for," Frog People said. "What next?"

Jase realized he'd be more likely to come up with an answer if he stopped staring at the door flap, and wondering when she'd come out again. He walked away, not caring for the moment where he went.

"If I have to kill the Olmaat to get the pouch, then I'll kill it," he said. "How do you kill an Olmaat?"

"You don't," Frog People told him. "Here in the Spirit World, there's nothing that can kill it. And in your world it's just a monster in a dream. I've got to say, she picked a good hiding place."

He sounded almost admiring, and Jase was reminded that to most of these people this was a political game—not the matter of life and death it was for him and Gima. And maybe his world, too.

For all their contempt for humans, these shapeshifters were pretty . . . small. Except for Raven, who at least was trying.

"If I could get hold of a weapon that could hurt the Olmaat, could I kill it?"

"Sure. But it would have to be a weapon that's both magic and real. And even if you had something like that, odds are the Olmaat would kill you before you could get close enough to use it."

Jase knew that too. The memory of otter-headed arms reaching into the cave swept over him, and his knees went *weak. But this was his grandmother's only chance, so he had to try.*

"Then I know where we're going."

"Really? 'Cause if you want me to guide you, it might be good if I knew too."

"I'm not sure you can guide me," Jase said. "We're going back to my car."

"Problem with that," Frog People said.

"What?"

"Your car's not in this world. And your consciousness is."

"I got hold of it once before," said Jase. "When I needed to."

But he'd had to get to his car to do it, with the body that now was lying against a rock pile drugged into sleep. With its ankles bound.

On the other hand Raven had said human dream walkers could split their consciousness. And he'd done it before.

Jase closed his eyes and reached inward with that delicate sense he'd been developing. If he looked at himself, felt himself, he wasn't all there. Jase groped for the rest of himself . . .

. . . and opened his eyes on the rain-wet forest of reality. He was dizzy from the drugs, cold and stiff, but his scratched fingertips stung from injuries he'd gotten in a dream—a dream that still lurked on the edge of his consciousness. He had to get back to his car. He had to get back to the Tesla. Now. But without completely waking up, without losing his hold on the dream world.

Keeping his eyes half shut, his breathing slow and steady, he started to rise, tripped and fell.

The belt, stupid.

The voice in his mind was distant, and he felt groggy, disoriented. The drug? Or because part of his mind was other where? He fumbled free of the belt and swayed to his feet. One step. Two. But the dream was beginning to fade. Jase let his consciousness fade with it, sinking down and away . . .

Jase opened his eyes. "I'm on the way," he told Frog People. A part of him could feel what was happening to that distant body, the pressure of earth against one foot then the other, even though he was standing still. Sudden cold washed over his cheek as a wet branch swiped that distant face, but he could feel his other self's determination to reach the Tesla. Jase just hoped his real body didn't go tumbling down the bluff, and break both their necks.

"But I have to find the spear too," he went on. "So I'd better get moving."

"Well, I can't guide you there," said Frog People. "I got no idea where your car is."

"That's OK. I do. At least, I think I do."

Assume the sinking sun in this world was in the same place as in his own. East was the direction he'd take in the real world to get back to his car, so Jase set off to the east.

Somewhat to his surprise, there were no bogs, no impassable thickets, no hook-flowers in his path . . .

Until he climbed out of a shallow dip, and found Otter Woman blocking the way.

"This is where I leave you." Frog People's voice was quiet, for him. "I'm a balancer, not a fighter."

"Neither am I!" He wondered where her football players were.

But the tiny frog was scrambling down the front of his jacket, so Jase put out a hand and let it hop onto his palm, then bent to let it leap off into the grass.

"This isn't the first time that frog's abetted my enemies." Hate burned in the old woman's eyes. "I'll deal with him. Right after I've dealt with you."

She began to shift before she'd finished speaking, shrinking, as golden fur sprouted and her cheeks puffed out to form the otter's face.

It didn't look friendly, but otters never attacked humans.

The otter shambled forward and launched itself with a hissing snarl.

Jase wasn't a fighter, but his survival instincts weren't as atrophied as he'd thought. He kicked the beast away and backed off.

"Hey, otters don't . . ."

Clearly, this one did. The sinuous brown shape was almost four feet long, and though its claws weren't that frightening, its teeth were designed for biting through shell.

At least on land it wasn't fast. It lumbered after him once more, and Jase darted back. He had to keep those teeth away from him. But how? If she kept trying, sooner or later—

It happened sooner, a bit of deadfall catching the back of one ankle and bringing him down.

Jase threw up his hands as the long muscular body surged over him, and caught the creature's neck just in time to keep those needle-sharp teeth from his throat. Powerful hind legs scrabbled against his belly, bruising, knocking the breath out of him, but its blunt claws couldn't penetrate his rain gear.

The front paws clawed at his wrists, but Jase didn't dare let go. He struggled to a sitting position and then to his feet, twisting the otter away from him so the kicking legs no longer connected, though its front legs still scratched his hands. It felt as if she was about to claw through to bone, but at least her teeth couldn't reach him.

Jase wrapped one hand in the loose skin at the scruff of her neck and held the twisting beast like a kitten as he lowered the other hand to fumble with his belt.

A tug on the buckle released the clasp, and he grabbed the belt and let the canteen slither off. The otter had to weigh thirty pounds, but Jase kept his grip, held it suspended in the air, and used his teeth to hold the buckle while he threaded the belt back through the opening and snugged it down to a small loop.

Even when he had the collar around her neck, he couldn't just let go of her.

Jase knelt and groped for the fallen tree he'd tripped over, feeling along the trunk till he found a place he could slide the free end of the belt beneath. He grabbed it when it emerged on the other side and pulled it through, only releasing the snarling beast when her head was pressed against the wood. He wrapped the belt around the narrow log and tied it off, then stood staring down at the trapped otter.

Blood seeped from dozens of deep scratches on his hands and wrists, and his breath sobbed in his lungs.

The otter clawed at the belt, snarling otter obscenities and glaring. She could probably shapeshift out of this in minutes, but that gave him at least a slight head start. His knees were so wobbly Jase feared he'd fall, but after a few steps he steadied into a run.

Would she come at him next in some other, stronger form? If that otter had weighed ten more pounds she might have had him, and the sting of deep scratches made the threat real.

Jase started looking as he hurried through the trees, and soon he saw a big dead snag with branches low enough to reach.

He chose the largest he could break, and threw his whole weight down on it to snap it off. It was crooked, and the nubs where twigs had sprouted dug into his palm, but it was better than no weapon at all.

Jase emerged into a patch of low scrub, where he could see the beach on his right and the ruins before him, though in this world the looming towers were only piles of rubble. He ran forward, threading the maze of bushes, watching for whatever might emerge to block his way, listening for something crashing behind him. If the eagle hadn't shrieked when it began its dive, it might have taken him completely by surprise.

As it was, Jase flung up his arms and ducked. Its claws nicked his scalp and raked two bloody furrows across one arm before it screamed again, and surged up in a rush of wind.

Blood dripped off his arm, and Jase felt hot streaks trickling down the back of his neck. These talons weren't the otter's blunt claws—if they fixed in him, that hooked beak could shred his flesh like a knife.

So don't let it.

Jase cocked his club like a batter at the plate, his gaze on the sky.

Even a stupid football player could learn. This time the eagle plunged in silence, the wind through its feathers almost a roar as it plummeted to strike.

Jase gripped his club and swung with all his strength—a fraction of a second early. The eagle lifted with a startled squawk, and he only caught it a glancing blow.

But that must have been enough, for as it circled, shrieking, Jase saw that it held one leg against its feathered breast.

It looped above him several more times, then flapped off to the west.

It was impossible to run and watch the sky and the ground at the same time, but Jase tried. He thought he knew what was coming next, and if he was right his ears would provide the best warning. Neither his club, or even the spear, if he reached it, would do anything against a swarm of bees.

He thought he could see the spear's icy glow below the ruins and gave up watching to run toward it, sacrificing safety for speed. But long before he reached it he heard the nerve-shaking whine of the angry swarm, far behind him at first, but growing louder with each passing second, each panting stride.

He'd lost enough elevation by now to leap down the shallow bluffs and reach the surf, which surged and withdrew to his left. Surf that could provide some protection, and he might get there before the swarm reached him.

He would never be able to reach the spear.

He'd been stung by bees before, and survived.

He could survive it again.

Jase ran for the spear, lungs laboring, as the swarm's snarl grew louder. A knife of fire stabbed his shoulder, and another the side of his neck.

He flung his club aside, and crushed the bee on his neck as he ran. Then the spear was before him, stuck tip down in the thin grass. Jase snatched it up and spun to run for the sea.

But the moment he laid hands on the spear, that faint blue glow burst into a blaze, and then receded into a bubble of light. The bees bounced off it, like raindrops off the Tesla's windshield.

They buzzed angrily around the fragile shell, the throbbing in his neck and shoulder reminding him of how much damage they could inflict. But they couldn't touch him, because he was sheltered in a bubble of magic . . . the same size as his car.

He, his body, had reached the Tesla in the real world, and somehow had the sense to close the doors.

The enemy couldn't harm him.

Jase stood, clutching the spear and gasping for breath.

The bees gave up throwing themselves against the glowing shield, flew into a seething mass, then morphed into the shape of a man. The eagle flapped down, landing awkwardly on one leg, then grew and melted into human form. A man, Jase noted, who stepped forward on two sound legs.

That hardly seemed fair—the cuts on his arm were still oozing. The football squad stopped outside the circle of light, but they said nothing. Otter Woman strode into the open meadow and stalked up to the protective bubble.

She carried Jase's belt in her hands.

"I will wrap this around your grandmother's throat, and pull till the last spark of life gutters out. I will— "

"No, you won't," said Jase. "Bear will stop you. I haven't broken the bargain."

The dawning realization on her face was almost funny.

"I haven't got any dust," Jase went on. "I don't have a sample hidden away to use later. And as long as that's true, you can't hurt Gima."

"But you're up to something!" Otter Woman proclaimed.

"Yeah, well, I never said I wouldn't try something."

"He didn't." The great bear trundled around one of the heaping piles of rubble. "So he's right. You can't harm the human woman. On the other hand, this little war'z beginning to get distracting. Disturbing. And Raven's right. Long as her human's fighting, she hazn' los-t."

Otter Woman threw out her arms in a gesture of furious frustration. "But if we turn Raven loose this fight will go on and on. She won't quit. She'll squirm and scheme till someone stops her. The humans are destroying our world. We have a right to defend ourselves."

Bear nodded. "So we finish it here. If the boy'll come out of that shell t' do it."

"Why should I come out?" Jase asked. "If I do I'll have to fight all three of them, and who knows who else. I won't quit, but I'm not crazy either."

He also didn't know how to get out, even if he was pretty sure how he'd gotten in.

Bear rolled his shoulders into a forward shrug, a little like Frog People's. "If you don' come out, you won't be able t' fight the Olmaat."

"*The Olmaat?*" *Jase looked around in alarm. "It's not here.*"

"*No!*" *Otter Woman exclaimed. "I control this Olmaat, and I won't bring it.*"

This Olmaat? Were there others? It was an appalling idea.

"*You will,*" *said Bear. "Raven's human haz earned the right to fight for her, so you'll bring your monster and give the boy a chanze to end it. One way or the other. For all of us.*"

Otter Woman opened her mouth to protest, saw that Bear's decision was made, and closed it. Her clear reluctance was a more persuasive argument for leaving the safety of his car than anything Bear had said. Goose Woman had told the truth. The medicine pouch was hidden in the Olmaat's heart. If Jase could kill it, take the dust, he could get his grandmother back.

If he *could kill it.*

He turned to Bear. "Can this spear kill the Olmaat?"

Bear looked closely, not at the weapon, but at the shell of light around it.

"*Yez, but you're going t' have to break it. Nothing else will release enough magic for the kill.*"

"*Break it?*" *Jase considered the strong shaft and honed stone point. It didn't look breakable.*

"*Shatter it,*" *the bear confirmed. "In th' Olmaat's body. Only way.*"

Otter Woman looked happier now. "I'll summon the beast."

She made no other move, but Jase knew the Olmaat was

being summoned. Horror swamped him at the thought of seeing that nightmare monster again.

He wasn't a fighter. Not with a spear, or anything else. He hadn't signed up for this shapeshifter war. But this was his only chance to get Gima back, and if she didn't awaken the war in his own family would blaze out of control.

If he could end the shifters' war, he might also earn a chance to end the war his father had started.

He might not be able to break the spear—but he could break the Tesla.

Jase took his right hand off the spear and made the familiar gesture of punching the Tesla's starter button. Listening with those other ears, he heard the faint, distant p-ping.

He groped until the fingers of a hand that wasn't in this world found the switch that lowered the Tesla's roof. The glowing circle around him disappeared.

"I'll fight," he said. "Bring on your beast."

○   ○   ○

He smelled it before he saw it, rotting fish and flesh, and an acrid choking stink that made him think of that brown cloud that had all but smothered the planet before carbon emissions were banned.

Bear laid down some ground rules, that this was between Jase and the Olmaat, with no one allowed to interfere. That this was Jase's one chance; if he lost and lived, he would never be allowed to return to the Spirit World again.

Never returning to the Spirit World sounded just fine to Jase, win or lose.

It was as dark now as the Alaskan summer night ever got, a dim gray light that dissolved the details of the Ol-

*maat's shambling shape. A bit like a gorilla, but with a
longer, thinner body, and legs that rippled bonelessly as it
strode forward. Piggy eyes glared above what looked like a
mountain lion's jaws, but it was hard to be sure under the
coarse black fur. Its wiggling fingers, surely more than five
per hand, were tipped with eagle claws.*

Jase's hands tightened on the spear . . .

. . . tightened on the steering wheel as the car lurched and
slithered down the track to the beach. The Tesla's wide tires
were good on sand, but the low-slung body scraped over every
rock. Part of Jase winced at each grating scratch, but the rest
of him was focused on his goal. Most of him was missing, but
the part that was here knew what it had to do.

*Jase summoned all his courage and took a step toward the
Olmaat. It opened its mouth and roared like an avalanche,
and he leaped back.*

*Laughter came from the sidelines, where Otter Woman
and her cohorts waited, and Bear gave an amused grunt.*

*Heat flooded Jase's face, but that animal roar had star-
tled him, shocked him.*

*Then the monster charged and Jase leaped away again,
swinging the spear wildly to fend it off.*

*The Olmaat wasn't as fast as he'd feared. He could stay
ahead of it, darting first to one side then the other, swiping
with his spear to make the monster keep its distance. If it
ever hooked those claws in him, he would die.*

Jase knew he hadn't turned, but the car was heading for the
surf again. He swore and wrenched the wheel around, feeling

how sluggish the Tesla was on sand, driving once more in the direction of the Olmaat rock. Half of him, half of the part of him that was there, thought he was crazy. The rest of him focused on two things: the great dark rock that was his target, and the glowing number on the control panel that tracked his speed.

45 miles per hour. The Tesla's engineers guaranteed a driver could walk away from any crash at 45 or less. But 45 mph was more than fast enough to shred carbon fiber and bend the light steel alloy, to crack a wooden staff and shatter a stone . . . Jase shook his head, shook off the alien thought. He was driving toward the bluff now. Was he going in circles? He corrected the car's course once more.

The Olmaat was driving him in circles.

Sweat ran down Jase's body, stinging in the cuts on his scalp and arms. Those cuts proclaimed the cost of getting within reach of the monster's claws, but he couldn't kill it from a distance. The mad thought of throwing the spear had occurred to him several times, but he'd never thrown a spear in his life. If he missed—and he'd almost certainly miss—he'd lose his spear, and the Olmaat could close and finish him.

If it kept running him around the beach, simple exhaustion would finish him.

To kill it, he would have to get close. Close enough for the claws at the end of those whipping arms to reach him.

Close enough to use the spear.

Jase gritted his teeth against a burst of panic, and started toward the Olmaat.

The rock appeared before him. This time, when Jase punched the accelerator, that view wasn't replaced by rolling waves or the low bluff. Steady, steady. He glanced at the speedometer: 45 miles per hour.

The Olmaat wasn't surprised by the change in his tactics. It kept darting away, trying to keep out of the spear's reach. And it was doing better at that than Jase was at dodging its claws. One swift swipe left his shirtsleeve in tatters. Another opened three shallow gashes above his knee.

The Olmaat's arms were too long for Jase's spear to reach its torso, and those arms moved too quickly for him to hit them. But its feet were slower.

He ignored the clothing that shredded on his body, the stinging pain, and the drip of blood above his knee. 45 miles an hour. 45. 45.

The rock was nearer.

Jase leaped in, changing the spear's direction at the last moment to thrust down at a furred, stationary foot.

The sweeping claws barely missed his head, and the spear was almost pulled from his hand as the monster jerked back, bellowing with rage and pain.

It limped back, blood staining the sand, and then stopped, waiting for him.

No more easy shots. No more running.

He took a breath and closed his hands around the spear. One step forward. Two. He darted to the right, dodged left, and lunged . . .

. . . the rock was in front of him, filling the windshield. Finally. Now. Jase punched the accelerator.

Four long gashes opened across his chest in a brilliant flash of pain, but Jase threw himself forward and thrust the spear into the Olmaat's body. Its anguished shriek shook the shaft in his hands, shook his world. For a horrible moment Jase thought he'd failed. Then the spear exploded, splinters raking his face and hands, and the world exploded with it.

CHAPTER 14

"Mr. Mintok? Mr. Mintok, our instruments show severe damage to your vehicle. Are you all right? Should I send medical assistance?"

Jase opened his eyes and found himself in the driver's seat of his car. What was left of his car. The windshield's safety glass had disintegrated, giving him a horribly clear view of the smashed hood.

"Mr. Mintok, I'm alerting Whittier Emergency Services now. If you can hear—"

"Don't!" The air bags were still deflating, so he couldn't see the control panel, but Jase knew he was talking to Travelnet. "Don't send anyone. I'm all right."

He thought it was true, though his face felt bruised where the air bag had slammed it. The Tesla's engineers had made good on their promise—he would walk away from this crash. And there was nothing in the Tesla, even smashed, that could explain the four long gashes across his chest to a medic.

"I'm OK," he told the dispatcher. "Really."

"If you don't want medical assistance, that's your choice," she said dubiously. "You appear to be conscious and coherent. But our diagnostics show severe damage to your vehicle. Are you certain you don't want medics? And if you don't want medical services, do you need us to send a tow truck?"

He would need a tow truck. And it would be expensive.

Not as expensive as crashing the Tesla.

"Not yet," Jase told the dispatcher. "I'd rather set that up myself. I want to take a look at the damage first."

"That's up to you, sir," the dispatcher said. "Do you have any further need of our services?"

"No, thank—wait! I can't find my com pod. It's probably around here somewhere." Jase was looking for it as he spoke. "But I don't see it. Would you call my home com unit and leave a message for my parents? Tell them the Tesla's . . ." *Wrecked.*

" . . . out of commission," Jase finished, though his throat was almost too tight to speak. "And that I can't find my com pod, but I'm going on to Gramps' anyway. I'll contact them from his house. Got that?"

"This conversation is being recorded," the dispatcher said. "I'll play it for them verbatim."

"Good," said Jase. "Thanks. That's all I need."

"If you're sure." The dispatcher sounded dubious.

"I'm sure," said Jase firmly. "I'm leaving now. I want to check the damage to my car."

And to check on something else that had caught his eye—a strand of brown leather dangling from a crack in the rock.

He went for the medicine pouch first, because he'd earned it, because it was easier than looking at his car.

It lay in a deep crevice in the rock that had opened when the car hit it. The pouch was dry and whole—how had they gotten it into the rock?

Clutching the medicine bag in his hand, Jase turned to face the rest of it.

The Tesla's hood was smashed back almost three feet; the

carbon fiber skin had ripped, its jagged edges fringed with fine white filaments. That might have been repairable. Or replaceable. The one good thing about his expensive insurance was that everything about the Tesla was fully covered. But looking at the impossible tilt of the tires, Jase was pretty sure the aluminum-alloy frame was sprung as well.

That too could be repaired, along with the broken fans, and the shattered pipes of the battery-cooling system from which coolant dripped like blood into the sand.

But if he replaced every component in it, it would no longer be his car. He might as well try to track down another Mark 14—and even if he could find one, it wouldn't be the same.

The Tesla was gone, and Jase's heart ached for the loss. But as much as that loss hurt, Gima's death would have hurt much worse.

No matter how much he'd loved it, it was only a car. And its destruction had saved much more.

Was this what they meant by dying with honor? If so . . . it sucked.

Jase made his way slowly up the bluff. He'd paid the price; he might as well get the benefit. Now, before anything else went wrong.

The sun hadn't risen. Without his com pod—which really had vanished—Jase had no idea what time it was, but the misty overcast was clearing off. The sky over the sea shimmered with luminous grays and blues, like the inside of a pearl.

When he reached the top, Jase looked out over the bay at the tidy lines of breakers and the dark slopes of the low hills.

He could hear the breeze in the trees behind him, feel it ruffling his hair—the parts that weren't matted with dried blood.

Every inch of his body ached and stung, particularly where

the bees had got him, and the cuts on his chest still bled. But he put that aside, and let his mind reach out to the ocean of air around him. This thin skin of atmosphere that circled the world gave life to everything that breathed. Jase drew it into his own lungs and gave himself up to it.

When he was certain he had the sense of it, he opened the pouch and pulled out a generous pinch of Atahalne's dust.

He understood more about magic now, and didn't bother with words. But as he cast the dust into the air he let the pain of breaking the Tesla into his heart, and willed for everything that was broken to mend, and heal, and be whole.

He was ready for the power surge, though this time it felt as if it was filling, inflating, lifting him up—so much that for a moment he thought his feet had left the ground.

But when Jase opened his eyes he was standing right where he'd been before . . . and northern lights danced in the sky above him.

You almost never saw them in the summer; conditions were wrong and the sky was too bright, even in the middle of the short summer "night."

These weren't the brilliant neon curtains that lit the winter darkness, but green and gold wisps that flickered across the gray vault . . . and then winked out.

Jase thought of Frog People and Goose Woman sensing a surge of ley power running all the way to the node, and his heart lightened. He thought of Otter Woman and the football squad's fury and grinned outright.

He thought of Gima's spirit, fleeing home through the dawn, and knew that no matter how high the price, it was worth it.

He turned, and almost ran into Raven.

Her glossy hair was tumbled, her stretchie rumpled and grubby, and her slender feet still bare. But she probably looked better than he did. Jase put up a hand to cover his shredded shirt, then let it drop because even a light touch hurt. He'd have to do something about those gashes eventually, but he preferred to put it off.

"I'm a mess."

"You were glorious." Her eyes were brighter than the northern lights. She stepped forward and reached up to touch his bruised face, then, very gently, pressed her lips to his.

After a moment Jase forgot about his cuts and bruises, and everything else. When he finally had to lift his mouth, in order to breathe, his arms were around her and she was pressed against his chest. He didn't even notice the pain till she stepped back, and blood-sticky fabric pulled at the cuts.

"Ow. No, wait. I didn't mean that. I—"

"I'm not going to sleep with you," Raven said. "You deserve, you've *earned* more respect than that. I won't treat you as a toy."

"Why not? This isn't like . . . I don't . . . Uh, what do you mean, *respect*?"

"You know what respect means."

"Yeah, but that doesn't mean you can't sleep with me! The reason I objected so much the first time was because you *didn't* respect me. You're supposed to respect the people you sleep with. It would be all right, now."

She was laughing.

"Right for you, maybe," she said. "But for me . . . No human ever fought for me before. No one ever saved me. And I like you, too. That's not something I'm used to with a human. I'm going to have to think about it."

"Which means you *can't* sleep with me?" Jase didn't see the logic of that at all.

"For now," said Raven firmly. "Besides, you really are a mess. You wouldn't enjoy it nearly as much as you think you would, particularly after you get over the joy of that healing and your aches set in."

They were beginning to set in now, though Jase thought he could ignore them given some encouragement. But despite that incredible kiss, Raven didn't seem to feel encouraging.

"I'm lucky they hid the dust in that particular Olmaat rock," he said, trying to sound suave and modest. "Or I'd be running all over Alaska looking for it."

Raven shook her head. "Jase, that pouch would have been in whatever rock you broke to kill the Olmaat. It was in all of them, and none, until you killed it."

"No!" Jase protested. "I'm not up for your weird physics. The ley is healed, right?"

"Flowing like crazy," Raven told him. "Down and through Denali, and out elsewhere. This will give me a great start on the next healing."

The next healing.

"You're leaving," Jase whispered. "You're going to leave right now."

"I don't have to leave *right* now," she admitted. "I've won, so Bear and the others will keep Otter Woman out of my way. But I do have to go. Since you're all right under the mess, it might as well be now."

He'd always known he wouldn't be able to hold her for long, but . . . "Will I see you again? Someday? When the leys are healed?"

Maybe she wouldn't respect him quite so much by then.

"Oh, you'll see me again," said Raven. "In your dreams."

She stepped forward once more. This time her kiss was softer, more a matter of promise than passion.

He could feel her growing lighter, less substantial in his arms. When he opened his eyes she was gone.

"Hey, before you go, where's my com pod?"

The only sound was the whispering wind.

Jase was halfway down the bluff before he realized that the medicine bag had vanished with her.

o   o   o

He hiked back into Whittier. He'd looked around the car again for his com pod, but it wasn't there. It was going to be interesting telling his parents that he hadn't lost it, it had turned into a beetle and flown away. If he didn't want to go through a lot of testing for a concussion he didn't have, he'd better claim he lost it.

His injuries weren't as bad as he'd originally thought, though the night clerk at the flash charge center stared when he came in. He found all the first aid supplies he needed on its shelves, and added a cheap stretchie to the growing pile, because the bloody rents left by the Olmaat's claws were a bit too obvious.

"Do you need some help, son?" the clerk asked as Jase swiped his charge card. "There's a med-tech down at the harbor. He won't mind waking up if he's needed."

"I can handle it," said Jase. "Thanks."

He'd bandaged and treated his accumulated cuts, stings and bruises, and eaten breakfast before the ferry arrived.

Jase took the ferry down the coast to Cordova, watching the sun creep over the mountains to the northeast, which told him it was around four in the morning. He missed his pod—but he was beginning to understand why some passengers stood at the rail and watched the view.

After some discussion with the ticket clerk, he hitched a ride on a mail boat that was headed for the resort and points south. In the early morning, he walked down the main street of the village his father had struggled so hard to leave behind. People were setting out for their boats or the resort. A few of them smiled or said hi as he passed, and even those who glared showed only their normal annoyance at seeing him.

They'd have to get used to that, Jase thought. They'd be seeing more of him.

On this sunny morning the front windows were open. Turning up the path to the house, Jase could hear his grandfather saying something about getting checked out anyway, and Gima's firm voice proclaiming, "I'm fine, you stubborn old coot! And you might as well stop pestering me. I've already said I'll tell you all about it when my witness gets here. And not a moment before. Not even you would believe this story without someone to back me up."

Jase would have hesitated to tell the story if she hadn't been willing to back him up, too. The thought of his grandfather's probable reaction made him grin, though his smile faded as he knocked on the familiar wooden panel.

His grandfather opened the door and stood, blocking the way. The lines on his face were deeper, harsher, but something about his expression looked softer than before.

"Father wasn't right," Jase said, before the old man could speak. "But he wasn't wrong, either. He took his own path, and he tried to build a bridge for anyone who wanted to follow him."

His grandfather's gaze swept over him, catching on the rent and bloodstained knee of his jeans.

"But he was wrong to try to blow up the bridge for people who didn't want to take that path," Jase went on. "I know that, now. I think the bridge needs to be made wider, so people can go both ways."

The bridge that had already been blown up? He wasn't saying this right. He was too tired, too confused to find the words. Jase reached up to rub his face, and his grandfather noticed the bandage on his arm. He looked at Jase and then—Jase could see it now—he looked at his grandson with a shaman's eyes.

Jase couldn't tell what the old man saw, but his eyes widened. His grandfather opened his mouth and then closed it, staring as if he'd never seen Jase before.

Astonishment gave way to an expression Jase hadn't seen for a very long time.

"Come in," he said.

And the door opened.

SHE HADN'T THOUGHT SHE COULD feel this way about a human. A human who wasn't a plaything, or a pet, but someone . . . real. Equal.

Someone she cared about.

Who'd have dreamed that confused boy would take the warrior path?

Oh yes, he'd see her again. And she probably owed Kelsa a visit too.

But that would have to wait, till the task was done.

Raven flew steadily south, with the rising sun behind her, and the medicine pouch flapping around her neck. It made flying harder, wasted energy, but she needed it. Not for the catalyst, but to keep the memory bright. Her kind wasn't good at remembering.

This would remind her, not only of him, but that humans could work, could heal, and with her guidance mend the damage they'd made. Kelsa and Jase had proved that, and with no enemies to stop them, the humans who would follow could complete that healing in peace.

No other human she guided would have to face the challenges they had. No other human would ever match the two of them.

But Raven had a world to heal. And now, only the doing remained.

o o o

The End

AUTHOR'S NOTE & ACKNOWLEDGMENTS

I find that science fiction and fantasy doesn't usually require me to write an author's note—because science-fiction and fantasy authors make stuff up. Most fantasy research consists of reading the ancient tales of whatever mythos you plan on stea—ah, borrowing, and that doesn't usually require an explanation. And science-fiction research (at least the way I do it) usually consists of tracking down articles in science magazines, which also doesn't need a lot of acknowledgment.

To write *Trickster's Girl* and *Traitor's Son,* I had to drive from Utah to Alaska—though I probably shouldn't say "had to" because the trip was a fantastic experience from start to finish. And even in *Trickster's Girl,* most of what Kelsa sees and does are things I saw and did (except for the stuff I made up), so there was still no need for an author's note.

Traitor's Son was another matter, largely because in this case I planned on "borrowing" from people who are still alive, and from a culture that still exists—which is always a tricky proposition if you're not a member of that culture. Writers often set stories in places that exist today, in the real world. But when a mystery writer sets her story in a small town and then realizes that the twists and turns of her plot require her to make the only son of the local sheriff a drug dealer, and that sheriff blackmails the mayor to keep his son from being prosecuted . . . that's when the mystery writer makes up a different name for her small town so she doesn't get sued . . . or even just make life difficult for the mayor and the sheriff's son.

My original plan was to get to Alaska, figure out which Alaska Native culture (even then I knew there was more than one) would suit my novel best, learn all I could about it, and then put that culture into my novel. But the more I learned about the five distinctly different Alaska Native cultures—all of which have their own language, customs, history, and incredibly ingenious technology—the more I realized that putting both the traitor and his son into an existing culture was not only fraught with pitfalls for an ignorant Caucasian from the Lower Forty-Eight, but that I might also end up inadvertently slandering some innocent lawyer and his kid.

So in the end, I decided to do what science-fiction and fantasy writers do best and made up my own tribe. The Ananut people and all their history, customs, and beliefs are pure fiction, invented by me. And I apologize to the Eyak of the Copper River for plunking my Ananut down in their territory.

The other bit of live research I did for *Traitor's Son* proved conclusively that writing novels is the best job in the universe: I got to go for a test ride in a Tesla Roadster. Zero to sixty in 3.7 seconds. My sincere thanks to Tara Flanagan and Mario Gambacorta of Tesla Motors in Boulder, who gave me all the information I needed and much more—including the weird things authors need to know, such as what would happen to that gorgeous car if you crashed it. As for the Tesla itself, I have only three words. Coolest. Car. Ever. (And zero to sixty in 3.7 seconds.)

Finally, I owe the state of Alaska an apology for . . . shortchanging it. In *Trickster's Girl,* my protagonist traveled from Utah to the Alaska/Canada border—and Kelsa is a nature girl who could appreciate and marvel at the gorgeous places she passed through. Jase, the protagonist in *Traitor's Son,* is *not* a nature boy. In fact, he's the kind of kid who can drive the Gle-nallen Highway, otherwise known as Glacier Alley, and not even see the ethereal ice floes that look like they're floating on the other side of the valley, because he's thinking about his car. (It's an amazingly cool car, but still!)

In a novel, you see the world through the eyes of your pro-tagonist. Jase is who he is, and that means I can't describe the Glenallen Highway, or the arching waterfalls of Keystone can-yon on the way to Valdez, or the enchanted fairy-forest where we camped outside Sitka, or whales half breaching out of seas as clear and clean as glass, or rain-shrouded fjords, or the soft *chee-chee-chee-chee-chee* sound bald eagles make when they're talking to each other, or the terns dipping daintily into the turquoise water of the Kenai River, or sunset at 1:25 a.m. in the campground outside Denali, or . . .

Once we knew we were going to Alaska, whenever my mother and I met someone who'd been there, we'd ask them what Alaska was like. They'd open their mouth and then get this funny look on their face and say, "Alaska is fantastic." And then they'd stop. Now that I've been there, I know that the problem isn't that there's not more to say, but that if you start trying to tell someone how beautiful, how wild, how open and clean and incredibly varied Alaska is, you end up babbling till your victim's eyes glaze over. If I had to pick just two words to describe Alaska, the first would be *grandeur* and the second *unearthly.* Aside from that . . . Alaska is fantastic. And through Jase's eyes, there's simply no way for me to do it justice.

HOW THE STORY BEGINS.

An excerpt from

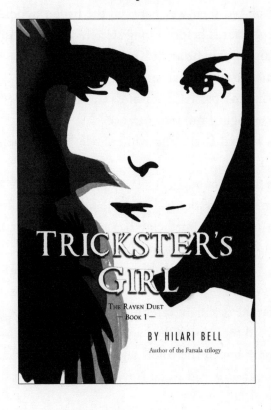

TRICKSTER's GIRL

THE RAVEN DUET
— BOOK 1 —

BY HILARI BELL

Author of the Farsala trilogy

Kelsa moved onward, both her light and her attention fixed on the rough floor. The glitter of crystals around its edge warned her about the first ice patch, but she slipped a little anyway.

"To the right," Raven murmured. "The floor rises. There's no ice there."

They picked their way between the frozen puddles for another dozen yards before a long stretch of floor coated with a thin gleaming skin brought Kelsa to a stop.

"I can't see any way around it."

"We haven't passed the bend yet," Raven protested. "We can still see light from the entrance."

Kelsa looked back. The white circle behind them looked plenty far to her.

"This is deep enough."

Raven stirred restlessly, but made no further protest.

Kelsa pulled the medicine bag out from under her shirt. Warm from the heat of her body, it felt as if it belonged to her—which was probably why Raven had insisted she wear it.

She sat the flashlight carefully on the floor and began untying the cord that closed the bag. "All right. What do I say?"

She only hoped she could say it in English instead of Navajo, though if it had to be Navajo he could probably coach her through it.

"You'll have to figure that out," said Raven. "It's your magic."

"What? You said all I had to do was drop a pinch of dust and say the incantation to activate it."

"That's exactly what you have to do." Raven's tone was utterly reasonable, though his teeth were beginning to chatter.

"But I don't know any incantations! This is crazy! You—"

"Don't get upset," Raven snapped, "or you won't be able to focus, and this is important! You were reaching out to the tree spirit when we first met. That's how I knew you could do this. Just reach out to the earth in the same way and tell it, persuade it, to heal!"

He sounded all too serious. Kelsa gazed around in exasperation. Even with her night vision and the flashlight, she couldn't make out more than a small portion of the floor and a bit of the wall beside her. But she could sense the space around her and the rock enclosing it, old and solid. The bones of the earth itself.

She didn't need to see. This wasn't a place of seeing.

Taking care not to spill the pouch, Kelsa sank down to sit on the cave floor. The stone was rough and cold under her butt—not at all comfortable. But that was part of this place too.

She let the cave seep into her senses: silent blackness and the scent of damp stone. It had a different aliveness from that of the trees, from anything in the world above. He'd been right. They hadn't been deep enough before.

She took some time to assemble all the words, but they felt right. Real.

"Bones of the earth, flowing liquid to the surface, crumbling to form the flesh of the world. You are so strong, nothing but time defeats you. Be strong now. Strong enough to forgive." ERB-1 loomed in her mind, in her heart. She'd been calling it dust, but what the pouch really held was sand, gritty between her fingers. Her father's ashes were mixed in with them. "Be strong enough to heal. Be strong!"

She scattered a pinch of sand over the cave floor as she spoke. The moment of stillness that followed was just long enough for her to feel monumentally silly—then all thought was wiped away by a shattering blow that set every bone in her body vibrating like a mallet-struck gong. The vibration went on and on, receding into darkness, pulling her with it.

Kelsa was lying on the tunnel floor when thought returned, lumps of stone pressing into ribs, hip, temple, and one sore knee. Her head ached fiercely.

"Ow! What the hell was that? Did you hit me?"

"No." Raven sat cross-legged beside her, looking far too comfortable on the hard stone. "You had a good connection to the ley, and some of the power lashed back through you. You were right. We were deep enough."

The smug smile was back.

"Frack you." She picked up the light, pulled herself to her feet, and started unsteadily out of the cave. Her headache lessened with each step, which it wouldn't if he'd hit her hard enough to knock her out. She was done with him, anyway.

Kelsa felt almost normal by the time she climbed back to the surface of the lava field, more shaken and angry than hurt. It took her several moments to notice that no one was on the trail anymore. The tourists were milling around the parking lot, waving their arms as they talked.

"What's going on?"

"I told you that nexus power frequently has physical manifestations." Raven was retying the cord around the medicine bag's neck.

She glared at him, then started back to the parking lot.

"Did you feel it! Biggest I ever—"

"Thought it would knock me right off my feet," an elderly woman was saying. "Would have, if I hadn't had my walking stick."

"I wonder if it did any damage."

"I wonder how big it was, on the Richter scale. Must have been at least a two."

Kelsa stared at the chattering crowd. Then she turned and waited for Raven. He was only a moment behind her.

"There was an earthquake? While we were in the cave? Why didn't I feel it?"

"You more than felt it." He took her arm and led her over to a picnic table. "Sit down. You're still pale."

"Did I . . . Did we . . . You're kidding!"

"I doubt it did much damage," Raven said. "Healing magic almost never does."

"But that's crazy!"

"You know, one of the main symptoms of crazy is denying or ignoring what your senses perceive. You can hardly deny you perceived that."

She couldn't deny it. Any more than she could deny she'd seen him shapeshift. Which meant . . .

"I could heal the tree plague? For real?"

"Not heal it," Raven admitted. "That will take a lot of people doing the same thing you're doing all over the planet."

"Is that what the other shapeshifters are doing?" Kelsa asked curiously. She had a lot of questions about shapeshifters, and he'd evaded most of them.

"No," Raven told her. "This is our first attempt. In fact, this is the first proof we've had that humans can heal the leys at all! But if you can strengthen and open this ley, all along its length, when the plague reaches the forests of the Northwest it will stop. And then, maybe, we can start pushing it back. If you succeed, your scientists will probably claim the bacterium couldn't survive outside the tropics. But if this ley isn't healed, strengthened, if the power doesn't flow along it like it does now in the nexus point you just blew open, then that plague *will* move out of the tropics."

"So." He held out the medicine pouch, dangling from the cord around his fingers. "For the final time, Kelsa Phillips, will you take up Atahalne's quest and finish the healing he started?"

She didn't have enough money to travel to Alaska. She didn't have time to get there and back before her mother missed her. She was only fifteen . . .

"Yes." Kelsa took the medicine bag and hung it around her neck once more. It felt right there. "But first, you're going to answer some questions."